MW01530578

FRESH

TEMPTATION

BARBOZA BROTHERS: BOOK ONE

by Reeni Austin

Copyright Reeni Austin, 2012

trademarks is not authorized, associated with, or sponsored by the trademark owners.

Edited by Laurie Laliberte of the Kindle All-Stars.

.

AUTHOR CONTACT:

Website: http://www.reeniaustin.com
Facebook: **http://www.facebook.com/ReeniAustin**
Email: **http://www.reeniaustin.com/contact**

CHAPTER ONE

"May I take your coat, sir?"

Victor forced a grin. "Sure." He handed his Italian suede coat to the coat check attendant.

Be a good sport, Victor told himself. He hated pretentious black tie dinners like these. This annual fundraiser was one of a handful of events he always attended in person instead of sending a colleague or simply issuing a large donation from his office. Tonight's ten-grand-per-plate meal was hosted by the Whitt Foundation, a respected non-profit humanitarian organization.

And since Victor's ex-fiancee was Alexis Whitt, he would have rather been anywhere else.

Their engagement had ended two months earlier—a year before their scheduled wedding date—when Victor caught Alexis in a compromising position with her personal trainer, Esteban. Such a cliche.

He blamed himself for a while. Maybe he spent too much time working and didn't lavish enough attention. He focused on maintaining the wealth he'd amassed at a young age as a successful investment banker. At thirty-one, Victor Barboza was one of the youngest billionaires in America. Quite a feat for a kid born on the wrong side of Guadalajara. Tonight he was here to support a worthy cause he believed in: one of the Whitt Foundation's efforts was building orphanages and schools in third world countries.

He had never told anyone the real cause for the break-up. Perhaps he should have, but he didn't. He had too much respect for Alexis's parents to subject the family to the frivolous gossip of Manhattan's upper east side.

Besides, petty snickering and sympathy weren't a part of his lifestyle.

Victor preferred to move on. Live and learn. No more spoiled little trust fund princesses for him.

He adjusted his tie and scanned the main ballroom for the handful of people he actually wanted to see in this crowd. In seconds he was approached by one business acquaintance, then another, most of them asking Victor's advice. Had he heard of some new hedge fund? What was the weakest growth stock to avoid this month?

It was only a matter of minutes, though, before one conversation took an awkward turn.

Tim Lundquist casually asked, "So the wedding's in April, correct?"

Bree Lundquist, in her green sequined gown, gave Tim a sharp elbow to the arm and cleared her throat. "The food smells divine, don't you think? I hear they hired a famous chef." She cackled and patted Victor's arm. "I hope we eat soon. I starved all week so I could look good in this dress but I may have to indulge tonight. So tell me, how does a man like you work so much but still find time to stay in such good shape?"

Victor chuckled. He was grateful for her swift change of subject. A good portion of this crowd was probably as oblivious to the latest upper east side gossip as Tim. He could tell by some random shy glances that there were surely rumors spreading, but he didn't much care. When this semi-uncomfortable event was over, it was back to seeing most of these people two or three times per year. That was something he certainly didn't miss about Alexis. She loved to find reasons for him to don a tux and mingle with "friends" of her family.

Victor chatted with the Lundquists for several more minutes when he felt a hand against his back.

"Barboza!" Douglas Whitt appeared at his side, jolly and boisterous as usual. "How's life in the penthouse?"

"Good." Victor smiled. The "penthouse" was an inside joke. Both he and Douglas Whitt came from meager beginnings before working their way to the top of the business world. And even though Victor would never be Douglas's son-in-law, he still considered Douglas a valued mentor and hoped to maintain a friendship.

Victor could've kicked himself for thinking any of Douglas's hard work and determination could have rubbed off on Alexis. Occasionally he thought about the day he met his former flame. She hooked him with, "My Daddy's the son of a poor Kentucky coal miner." Her intentions were so obvious now. Marry a rich, handsome bachelor who'd make Daddy proud, while elevating her social status. If there was anything else she cared about, Victor sure didn't know what it was.

Douglas handed Victor a glass. "Bourbon. Thought you could use it."

"It's that obvious?" Victor took the drink and immediately brought it to his lips.

The robust gray-haired man shrugged and inched closer, his voice quiet. "Listen, if it weren't for my wife I'd never attend another one of these God-awful shindigs. We have an agreement. She gets to dress up and throw a fancy party for all her friends, and I get drunk enough to pretend I wanna be here."

Victor almost spit out his drink, laughing.

"It's true," Douglas said. "We could raise more money if we didn't have to use the best caterers in town or rent this ballroom." He sighed. "Oh well. C'est la vie. When are we having that lunch we always talk about?"

"Uh…soon."

"Don't worry, son. I'll not try to sway you to reconsider." Douglas gave him a knowing smirk.

Victor was stunned that the old man brought it up so casually. He knew from a few quick email exchanges that Douglas was disappointed about the broken engagement. He could also tell Douglas had no idea Alexis had cheated. The two men had become fast friends, and Douglas welcomed humble, hard-working Victor into the family as his own son, hoping he would be a good influence on his daughter. And perhaps, subconsciously, that was why Victor had avoided Douglas's friendly invitations for lunch or drinks after work. He would take no chances on being persuaded to give the woman a second chance.

But there was a murky place deep inside Victor's heart that still longed for Alexis. Aside from her pampered rich-girl tendencies, she was actually a smart, lovely woman six years his junior and fresh out of law school. And she was undeniably hot. Long auburn hair. Sparkling blue eyes. Legs for miles. She would have no trouble landing another eligible billionaire in no time. Landing one who would so easily win Douglas's approval again…that would be tricky.

Victor took another sip of his bourbon and looked Douglas in the eye. "Soon, then. This week, maybe next."

"Wonderful." Douglas smiled and slapped Victor's shoulder. "Now if you'll excuse me, there are some stuffy socialites I need to see."

A few minutes later, as Victor chatted absently with people he'd never met before, the lights dimmed for an instant. A voice rang out over the speakers. "Ladies and gentlemen, please take your seats. Dinner will be served in five minutes. Your table assignment can be found on your ticket."

Victor pulled his ticket from his pocket to see he was assigned to table number eleven. He briefly glanced around the room for his ex-fiancee, then breathed a sigh of relief. He hadn't seen her all night. With any luck, she was keeping her distance and he could go the entire night pretending she didn't exist.

There were ten chairs at table eleven. Victor sat in one of the four that was vacant. An elderly couple quickly filled two of them. The guests at the table commenced with small talk. The chair to Victor's left was still empty when the wait staff began distributing the first course.

And then, seemingly from out of nowhere, the empty chair moved.

Unconcerned, Victor turned to greet the new guest. He closed his eyes for a moment and smothered his groan before it could leave his throat.

Alexis, of course. Auburn hair clipped atop her head, hanging down in deliberate ringlets. Long black dress, cut low at the chest, with a slit from her heels to her thigh. In other words, she was gorgeous.

But she was still the coddled heiress who cheated on him.

"Hello, all." Alexis's tone was perky as she addressed her table mates. "I hope we're all having a lovely evening so far."

A few people returned her greeting. Victor immediately decided to be as quiet as possible. He saw the awkward glances from a few others at the table who obviously knew of the break-up and probably wondered if they were now back together. When the appetizer was placed in front of him seconds later, he said, "Bourbon, please," to the server.

Alexis was silent for a moment as the others at the table talked amongst themselves. Then she cleared her throat. "So you won't talk to me? Or look at me?"

"I'm here to support a good cause. That's all."

"You could at least be civil."

"I *am* being civil."

She edged closer and lowered her voice. "Come on. There'll be a scene if you ignore me. You know people are watching us."

Looking straight ahead, he answered through gritted teeth. "Then perhaps you shouldn't have sat down next to me. Or had us both assigned to the same table."

"Well…I thought maybe you wanted to talk to me. Why else would you be here tonight?"

"I already told you. To support a good cause."

Her silence conveyed her disappointment loud and clear. But Victor went on, striking up a conversation with the couple sitting next to him.

After numerous attempts to get his attention, she interrupted him mid-sentence with a loud whisper in his ear. "Please talk to me."

Knowing her too well, he closed his eyes and leaned a bit closer. *Might as well get it over with.* "What is it?"

"I'm sorry I had to do this. You ignore my calls. I need to speak with you."

"Then get on with it."

She stammered in response to his sharp tone. "I just… think…we should give it another shot. I…" She gulped. "I was wrong. It'll never happen again."

His head shook. "We're finished. I know who you really are now."

"No, you don't."

"Yes I do. Trust me. This little stunt you pulled tonight is exactly what I'm talking about. You're so selfish; you'll do anything to get your way." He finally made eye contact with

9

her, leveling his glance just enough to show the woman he could not be charmed by her loveliness. Yes, she was an auburn-haired vision to behold but he wouldn't be made a fool twice. "I only came here tonight out of respect for your family and this organization. I would walk out of here right now, *chica*, but that would only cause you and your family embarrassment. You want people to talk about us tonight and think we're back together but I don't care what they think."

Alexis pursed her lips, hoping to contain her tears. She remembered when he used to call her, "*mi amor*." And now, "*chica*?" It rolled off his lips in such a tawdry fashion. "You're making a mistake."

"Well, you made one first." Victor scooted his chair as far from her as possible and struck up a new conversation with the couple sitting beside him.

After several unsuccessful attempts to get his attention again, Alexis excused herself from the table. Victor didn't turn around to see where she went.

* * *

Cara Green held her cell phone at her thigh and tried not to let her supervisor see she was reading a text message. Luna Lee Catering had a strict policy against cell phone usage, and as much as she needed this weekend job, she had to know if her three-year-old son, Isaac, was all right.

The text message from her mother read, "In ER right now. Temp 103."

Cara's eyes welled up as she slid the phone into her pocket. She wanted to stay home and take care of him today, but it wasn't possible. Between her three jobs, she would soon have enough money to pay the outrageous co-pay for the tonsillectomy Isaac desperately needed. She mustered a grin and tried not to think about how miserable and fussy he had been since yesterday. When she left the house for work today, he launched his warm little forehead against her chest, crying for her to stay. As long as she didn't picture his sad face, she was fine.

Isaac was prone to ear, nose, and throat infections. The doctor made it perfectly clear that a tonsillectomy was inevitable. "Simple procedure," he said, "kids recover fast." The doctor went on and on trying to convince her, but Cara was already convinced.

If only her insurance company wasn't such an asshole.

Trying to save money, Cara swallowed her pride and moved in with her mother. So far, it wasn't nearly as bad as she had feared. She was just another of the many people she knew who had to move back in with their parents after layoffs, divorces, inability to find a job. For Cara, being a twenty-seven-year-old single mom while living with her mother was a nightmare come true. But she tried to stay positive. She just knew she would get another public relations job once the economy turned around. This life of working three jobs and barely spending time with her son would end once she had a nest egg saved up. During the week, she was a receptionist at a ramshackle construction company that she was pretty sure doubled as a front for a money laundering scam. On the weekends, she worked for Luna Lee Catering when they needed her. And if that wasn't enough, she helped an old high school friend, Marcy, with her new office cleaning business in the evenings.

This week, Cara had seen Isaac a total of twelve hours. And for most of those hours, he was asleep with his latest sinus infection.

On the bright side, this was the swankiest party Cara had seen in a long time. The staff had already been alerted that there would be plenty of trays of goodies to take home tonight. Leftovers were a blessing for her bank account, but a curse for her waistline. Since taking this job, she had gone from a size ten to a size fourteen, but that was the least of her concerns. She ate what she could, when she could. Tonight, she and some of the other servers had already polished off several small trays of heavy hors d'oeuvres, courtesy of the manager.

And her pants felt even tighter.

She chuckled to herself and popped a mini-quiche into her mouth, from the tray she was preparing. They were going to make a delicious breakfast tomorrow.

She was just about to start on the next tray when her supervisor, Keith, walked in.

"Need you out front, Cara." He groaned. "Sandy just went home with the stomach flu."

"Great." Cara nodded, praying silently that she hadn't already been exposed to new germs to bring home to Isaac.

Seconds later, she walked out of the kitchen with an empty tray and started to clear dishes from tables full of guests who were finished with the first course. As usual, she was amazed by the excess surrounding her. *Why do women need to wear prom dresses to raise money to fight poverty?* This was *so* not her scene. Rich people eating rich food, having boring conversations about rich things. Most of them didn't make eye contact with her when she asked, "May I take this?" They just nodded and went about their evening, chatting with the people beside them. She smiled despite their arrogance. Some of the men wore cuff links that surely would have paid off her entire credit card debt.

On her third round of cleanup, a few of the guests spoke to her, making polite small talk.

An elderly woman touched her arm. "Could you please tell me the name of tonight's chef, dear? This food is simply divine."

"Um…" Cara shut her eyes tight for second, trying to remember. She had only heard it once, during the staff meeting before set up, and she was distracted with the task of hiding her cell phone. There was indeed a fancy chef on staff that night. From what Cara understood, he supplied the recipes and hung around in case one of the guests wanted to pay him their compliments. She saw him for approximately five seconds before he headed off to the terrace for the evening to smoke cigarettes. But she suddenly remembered. "Um...Andrew Trafalgar!" She calmed her voice and repeated herself. "Yes, Andrew Trafalgar."

The woman turned to her husband, nodding. "We'll have to keep him in mind, won't we?" She smiled and gave Cara's hand a warm pat. "Do give him my compliments, please. The name's Betsy Kisch."

Cara grinned, hiding her tightly clenched teeth. "Yes. Betsy Kisch. I'll remember." *Sure, like I have nothing better to do than to pay your compliments to that jackass doing nothing but sitting on his ass outside?*

Betsy turned to the handsome man on her other side. "Smashing first course, wouldn't you agree?"

The young, dark-haired man spoke dramatically. "Absolutely, Bets. *Smashing.* How in the world did you read my mind?" Quickly, he cocked a brow and gave Cara a wink that made her chuckle.

Betsy Kisch gave him a playful slap on his wrist and burst into laughter. She knew she was being mocked.

Appreciating his sarcasm in the midst of this stuffy crowd, Cara asked a question just as a gorgeous redhead took the vacant seat beside him. "Sir, would you like me to forward your compliments to Mr. Trafalgar as well?"

"Sure. Victor Barboza." He gave the redhead a short, sideways glance, then looked up at Cara. "But I won't be needing the services of a chef or a caterer anytime in the foreseeable future. No big events coming up."

The redhead stared straight ahead. "That's enough, Victor."

Cara let out a nervous giggle, her wrist aching from the tray of dirty dishes she supported with one hand. Tension was unmistakable between these two strangers. "Okay then. I'll pass the compliment along."

As soon as the words left her mouth, her phone vibrated in her pocket and her smile disappeared.

Isaac.

Tears filled her eyes. *I'm the worst mother in the world.* If only she weren't so desperate for this paltry paycheck she would have taken her sweet, sick toddler to the emergency room herself. She briefly scanned the room, sickened by the decadence. These people had no idea how easy their lives were compared to hers. Surely their children wanted for nothing, especially something as simple as medical care for a sinus infection.

Since the room was noisy and the people at this table seemed nice, Cara looked around for her supervisor. She then made a split-second decision to look at her phone.

She forced a big, fake smile, hoping they wouldn't notice her watery eyes. "Is it okay if I set this tray down on the table for a sec?"

Victor returned her smile. "Sure, honey. Take all the room you need." He took the tray from hand and placed it directly in front of him.

"Thanks." Cara didn't notice the redhead's jealous glare as she pulled her phone from her pocket. She looked down at her mother's message, which said, "Surgery Monday morning. Call soon."

A few tears escaped Cara's eyes and she wiped them away. If a doctor deemed it to be an emergency, the cost would be completely covered, either by her insurance or by one of the free hospitals in the area. And even if that fell through, she would find a way to pay for it herself. A hefty monthly payment plan, a new credit card, another job. Whatever it took. She felt a sense of relief, knowing Isaac would soon be back to his fun-loving self.

She took a deep breath and reached down for the tray. "Thanks."

Victor's eyebrows crinkled. "Everything okay?"

She grinned. "It will be."

The redhead stood just as Cara lifted the tray. "Was that a cell phone I just saw?"

Shit. Cara's tone was sheepish. "Um…yeah."

Victor shot the redhead an angry look. "Alexis, don't."

Alexis walked around his chair and looked Cara in the eye. "We were assured the staff wouldn't spend their evening on their cell phones. It's very unprofessional and this is an expensive event."

Cara felt a giant knot form in her stomach. "I'm really sorry. I know I could get in trouble but I have a three-year-old in the emergency room. He's really sick."

The guests at the table were now looking at Cara, their mouths gaping.

Betsy Kisch spoke up. "Oh dear, what's wrong? Is he all right?"

Alexis shook her head. "You're here, working, instead of taking care of your sick son?"

Cara's mouth dropped open. "Yes, as a matter of fact." Her fear quickly turned to anger as she looked in Alexis's judgmental eyes. "You know, some of us weren't born with silver spoons in our mouths. Some of us have to work hard for a living, even when we have sick kids at home."

Alexis scoffed. "Yeah, whatever." She turned on her heel and scurried away, her long dress flapping against her perfectly toned calves.

"That's just great." Cara sucked her bottom lip between her teeth and closed her eyes, hoping the tears wouldn't come. She knew she would lose her job over this.

The people at the table all spoke at once. Cara was too shaken to discern any of their words. She simply reached down for the tray, opened her eyes, and headed back to the kitchen as fast as her feet would allow. She was almost there when she heard someone following her.

"Hey." Victor put a hand against her back. "I'm so sorry about her."

Cara paused to look in his eyes. "That wife of yours…" She shut her mouth. *Maybe you won't get fired. No need to mouth off and make your situation worse.* She grunted and walked on through the swinging kitchen doors.

Victor followed her inside. "She and I aren't together. She's a fucking bitch. I'll talk to your manager. Alexis is probably angry because I'm ignoring her and she thought I was flirting with you. She's really selfish."

Cara let out a cold chuckle and sat the tray on top of the counter. "Yeah well, maybe I'm better off. I need to go check on my son anyway."

"Is he okay?"

"He will be."

"Is there anything I can do?" Victor's brown eyes were full of compassion. "Let me make this right."

Cara couldn't look in his eyes for long. She sensed his sympathy, and she didn't want it. She stared off at the wall. "No, please. You wouldn't understand."

"Come on, try me. At least tell me which emergency room." He put a gentle hand on her shoulder.

Tears suddenly flowed freely down her face. His touch sent her over the edge, and she wasn't sure why. Maybe deep down, she really did ache for his sympathy; for the touch of a handsome man who offered help of some kind. But she thought again about the sequins and shiny jewelry flaunted in that ballroom. At a ten-grand-per-plate dinner. It was shameful, and she wanted no part of it. No, her desperate situation would make both her and Isaac stronger; she always found a way to get through. She shook away from Victor's grasp, sniffling. "Please don't. I really need to go."

Cara ran to the back room to retrieve her purse from her locker. Victor didn't follow. Soon she was driving home, leaving her catering job behind. She no longer cared whether or not she was fired.

Maybe that rich bitch was right, she thought. Maybe she should've been taking care of her son instead of working tonight.

CHAPTER TWO

It was Monday morning and Victor was tired. He had spent the last two nights since the fundraiser tossing and turning in bed, feeling sick about the woman Alexis had gotten fired.

Why couldn't Alexis just let it go? When she came back to the table and learned how unpopular her decision was, she apologized. Claimed she wasn't jealous. She was only trying to look out for her family's best interest and she got carried away.

Victor had never hit a woman in his life, but he secretly wished one of the other women at the table would have smacked Alexis. Betsy Kisch was quite vocal with her outrage. In her younger days, the feisty socialite probably would have taught Alexis a lesson or two. The thought almost made him smile…until he thought about that woman again.

He could tell by the way the now-fired woman spoke to Alexis that she was as disgusted with the event as he was. Damn, he hated himself for attending those showy dinners, but at least he tried to keep his attendance to a minimum and make sure he donated as much as possible.

Why didn't he ask her name? He now kicked himself. All he knew was the name of the company for which she had worked: Luna Lee Catering. And so far, calling every possible number for this company had resulted in him leaving at least ten unreturned voicemail messages.

But it was now Monday morning. Time for people to check their voicemail and call him back regarding his inquiry. He simply had to track down this woman and rectify the situation.

Victor's first stop was his assistant's desk. "Mornin' Gary."

"Morning Mr. Barboza," Gary said. As usual, he was bright and perky, wearing his headset with a smile like he'd been happily waiting there at attention for hours by then.

Victor grinned. "Hope you had a good weekend. Say, did you get my email?"

"About the woman you're trying to find?"

"Yes. Could you—"

"On it. Waiting on a call back from the receptionist. Said as far as she knew they hadn't fired anyone over the weekend, but it's early."

Victor let out a heavy sigh. "Okay."

A half hour later, Victor was about to head to a meeting when Gary rang his phone. "Yes?"

"I have Stacy at Luna Lee on hold. She said there were two people fired over the weekend and another quit. She thinks they all have at least one child. Could you give me a physical description to narrow the options?"

"Sure," Victor said. "Blond hair, green eyes, glowing skin. Lovely girl. Breathtaking, really."

It was only when Gary let out a small chuckle that Victor realized perhaps he remembered a little too much about her. And he knew how it sounded, like he had an entirely different agenda for tracking down this beautiful woman. But Victor didn't care what anyone thought. He simply had a situation to fix. A woman with real problems had touched his heart and reminded him of his own mother. That's all it was. So what, she had a stunning appearance? He wanted to help her even if she didn't. Perhaps he wouldn't have remembered her so vividly, but he certainly would have wanted to help. Victor cleared his throat and continued, this time calming his enthusiasm. "I have no idea how long her hair was. She had it pulled up in a bun. Don't know if that helps."

"*I guess we'll see. Let me click over.*"

Victor's heart raced as he waited for his answer.

Gary's voice quickly returned. "Okay. Sounds like you're looking for Cara Green. That's 'Cara' with a 'C.' She lives in Newark. I have her address and phone number."

Again, Victor stifled his enthusiasm. "Great."

"Would you like me to have accounts payable cut her a check? It probably wouldn't be hard to find her bank account and wire some money."

"Just give me the address and phone number. I'll take care it from there."

* * *

"He's doing fine," the nurse told Cara. "The doctor will decide if he needs to stay overnight. Usually kids with severe infections stay a little longer but I can already tell he's a tough one."

Cara nodded and stroked the side of Isaac's cheek. He had just fallen asleep after his second popsicle. "Yeah, he's tough. I didn't expect him to have so much energy so soon."

"Little ones recover quickly. You'll probably have to fight for the next few days to get him to rest. My daughter was ready to get on the jungle gym the next day."

Cara laughed. "I'll do my best."

When the nurse left the room, Cara was sure she'd start crying again. But watching her little guy sleep so peacefully warmed her heart. It had been days since he slept without snoring.

"Sorry this had to wait so long," she whispered as she bent forward to kiss his cheek. Then she took a long, deep breath before deciding to leave the room to find a vending machine in response to her growling stomach. "I'll be back in a minute." She gave the slumbering boy another kiss before turning around.

Her feet had just touched the hallway outside the room when a man sitting on the opposite wall stood up, startling her.

"Cara?" he asked. "Cara Green?"

"Um…" It took her a few seconds to remember how she knew the tall, dark stranger. But when she remembered, she couldn't stop her groan. "You. How did you find me?" As soon as the words left her mouth, she rolled her eyes at her own stupidity. *Of course he found me*, she thought. *Rich people can do anything.*

Victor maintained her eye contact as he reached behind him to pick up a large gift bag. "I'm not stalking you. I was just concerned. And I brought you a few things." He stepped forward and handed her the bag. "It's not much. A stuffed animal and a care package from the gift shop."

With hesitation, Cara took the heavy bag, immediately looking inside. Not much? It was filled to the top. "You didn't have to do this."

"I wanted to. Please take it." He covered her hand with his, tightening her grip on the handle.

Tears filled her eyes. "It's very generous. Thank you."

He looked into her eyes, waiting another moment before removing his hand from her soft skin. "Listen, what happened to you the other night was wrong. I—"

"I'd like to forget about it if you don't mind."

Victor nodded. "Sure. I understand. So, do you," he paused, trying to read her blank expression, "need a job?"

"No. Absolutely not." She squared her shoulders and shook her head. "I have a job."

"Yeah. Two jobs, from what your mother tells me."

"You spoke to my mother?" *Oh Lord, what does this man already know about me?*

"Yes. That's how I tracked you down." He smiled. "Nice lady. Invited me in for coffee. Said she was coming by the hospital after she filled a few orders. So, she runs a bakery out of her house?"

Cara's mouth dropped. "Wait a minute. I don't even remember your name and you've already had coffee with my mother?"

Victor chuckled and extended his hand. "Victor Barboza. Nice to meet you. Again."

She shifted the gift bag to her other arm, smirking as she took his hand. Careful not to gaze too deeply into those smoldering brown eyes…"Cara Green."

"I know."

She let his hand go as quickly as she had taken it. "Well, Mr. Barboza, it was nice to see you again but I'm sure you have to be somewhere." Right then, her stomach produced a loud growl. Warmth instantly rushed to her cheeks. She rolled her eyes and continued. "Seriously…just…thank you." She turned around to go back into her son's room.

"Wait, if you're hungry there's food in the bag."

"Thanks."

"Can I see your boy? Isaac?"

Cara stopped with her hand on the door. What the heck did this stranger want with them? "Only for a minute. He's resting."

Victor followed her into the room and stopped beside Isaac's bed, smiling. His voice was quiet. "Spunky little thing, I'll bet. It's probably killing him to be sick. Patty said he loves to go to the park."

"Yeah." *He's already on a first name basis with Mom?* Cara's eyes narrowed at the handsome man who now stood over her son's bed, peering down at him as if they were old friends. She couldn't wait to find out just how much "Patty" had told Victor. Or why. "Look, I appreciate the gift and I know my son will too. But we don't need your pity. We can take care of ourselves."

"I'm sure you can. But sometimes a person just needs to accept the kindness of strangers." He turned to her, flashing a grin. "You know, I haven't always had it easy. My brothers and I grew up with a mom who struggled to put food on the table and clothes on our backs. Please, just let me be nice to you for a moment. It's the least I can do after what happened."

Cara steeled herself. In her experience, people like him usually wanted something in return for their kindness. What did she possibly have to offer someone like him? She was a down-on-her-luck single parent who couldn't even afford a routine surgery for her son.

Maybe he just felt guilty. She and Isaac were a charity case and he had a hero complex. That had to be all it was.

"Mr. Barboza, I do really appreciate your kind thoughts and the gift." She motioned vaguely to the door, hoping he would take the hint and leave.

"Very well." He gave Isaac a long look before reaching into his pocket and turning to her. He handed her a card. "If you need anything, please call. Especially if the insurance company turns down your claim. I mean it."

Mom told him way too much. "Yeah. Sure."

Their eyes met for a few seconds. Long enough to make

Cara's breath catch in her throat. Hopefully he hadn't noticed.

He gave her one last nod and left the room without another word.

Cara sighed with relief, now aware she had forgotten to exhale.

She would probably fantasize about him for a few weeks, and why wouldn't she? It wasn't every day a kind Latino hunk muscled his way into her life. But there was no sense letting him overstay his welcome. Besides, she saw the kind of woman he used as arm candy. Victor Barboza would make a nice story to tell her friends. Maybe give her a dream or two to keep her warm at night. And for that, she was grateful.

She marveled at Victor's kindness as she searched the gift bag, estimating the cost of the items in her mind. There were designer shoes in Isaac's size, toys, first aid supplies, small packages of gourmet food. He had to have spent at least two thousand dollars, not including the cost of the glittery silver bag that held the gifts.

She took some crackers and stashed the rest in a large drawer for safe keeping. Then she made sure Isaac was still sound asleep before she went to the hallway to call her mother.

Patty answered frantically on the first ring. "*Is he still doing all right? I've been trying to get there for hours but I've had a million things to juggle.*"

"Isaac's fine. I heard you had a visitor?"

"*A visitor?*" She paused, then giggled. "*Oh, you mean, Victor.*"

"Yes. What did you tell him?"

She sighed. "*I don't know, sweetie. He had a lot of questions about you two. I answered them. No big deal.*"

"No big deal?" Cara took a second to remember all the things he'd mentioned in his short visit. "Let me see. He knew about me having two jobs. He knows Isaac loves to play at the park. Knows his shoe size. And he thinks you run a bakery out of your house? Since when does making a few specialty cakes mean you run a bakery?"

"He must have been confused about that."

"What about the rest? He's a total stranger, Mom! I hate to think what else you probably told him."

"He's a charming young man who's taken an interest in you. You don't need to be so melodramatic."

"He hasn't taken an interest. He just feels guilty because his girlfriend got me fired from Luna Lee the other night."

"Well, he didn't say anything to me about having a girlfriend. It's hard to imagine why a man like him couldn't have any woman he wants."

"Exactly." She let out a sad sigh.

"Don't be so hard on yourself. Give the guy a chance."

"Mom, it's not like that. He felt guilty and wanted to do a good deed. Don't make it out to be more than what it is."

"Is this because of the weight you've gained? Because I've always heard Mexicans like their women a little bigger."

"Mom!" Mortified, Cara glanced around the hallway as if someone could hear her mother's crude statement. "It's a lot of things. A rich guy like him with a single mom from Newark? It's ridiculous." As she finished her sentence, she heard Isaac crying. She rushed into the room to tend to him. "I gotta go, Mom."

"Are they letting Isaac come home today?"

"Don't know yet. Bye."

As Cara soothed her aching son, she shoved the thought of Victor Barboza to the back of her mind. It was too silly to entertain for long.

* * *

Victor had one hand on the wheel as he weaved through traffic on his way back to the office. Usually, his office was his favorite place to be, but on this sunny day he fantasized about taking a well-deserved day off, driving outside the city. Maybe somewhere upstate. Someplace where the grass was green and the air smelled fresh.

And he wanted someone to share it with. His mind's eye kept flashing back to Cara. Damn, she looked even more beautiful with her hair down. Thick blond hair, green eyes. The prettiest porcelain skin he'd ever laid eyes upon. He had to find a reason to see her again.

Cara was so different from the women he usually dated. She was hard-working and willing to sacrifice for her child. The polar opposite of stuck-up princesses like Alexis. No more of that for him. If their interrupted engagement had taught Victor anything, it was how much he didn't want another woman like her.

Victor laughed at himself. He heard his brother Ramon's voice inside his head. *If any one of us is going to marry someone like Mama, it's you.*

It was nothing to be ashamed of. The Barboza brothers— Victor, Ramon, and Armando—wouldn't be where they were today without their mother's sacrifice. She worked three jobs so her sons could concentrate on school. Unlike some of their friends who were already working the farms outside of town by age eight.

It had been a long time since the image of any woman had stuck with him like Cara Green. And that included Alexis Whitt. Sure, Alexis was easy on the eyes and she could hold a decent conversation. But Cara had fight. She was willing to roll up her sleeves and do her best for her son.

What if Alexis somehow lost everything? And, God forbid she have a child. Alexis wouldn't know how to take care of herself, let alone another person.

Cara deserved to be paid back for her labor. Patty said she hadn't seen her daughter go on a single date since she moved in with her six months earlier.

I need to find a way to see her again, Victor thought. He could already tell from the fire in her eyes that she had pride. Just like Mama. She didn't want a handout.

But she at least needed a better job.

He came to a stoplight and took out his phone, where he'd made a few notes. Then he called his assistant.

Gary's tone was chipper as usual. "Yes, Mr. Barboza?"

"Hey. I know I'm late for a meeting but—"

"It's okay. I rescheduled everything for tomorrow like you requested."

"Good. I need you to do some research. Doyle Construction. Morristown. See if we have a connection to anyone there." He smiled. "They have an employee I wanna steal."

CHAPTER THREE

"What a long day." Marcy exhaled in relief as her foot hit the gas pedal. "Already feels like it should be Friday, not Tuesday."

Cara closed her eyes and let her head fall back against the headrest. "Tell me about it. I got a glass of cheap wine waiting for me after I make sure Isaac's okay."

"Isn't your mom taking care of him?"

"Yeah, but she needs to sleep. Last night we took turns waking up every couple of hours to make sure he took his medication." Cara yawned.

"Aw, the poor little guy. You really didn't need to come out and help me clean tonight. You should've just stayed home with him."

Cara was too tired to cry. "I can't. I need the money. Heck, I'm down a job now. I don't know how I'm gonna pay my cell phone bill this month."

Marcy shook her head and gave her friend's knee a reassuring pat as she drove. "Let me know if I can help. I can give you an advance on the money I'll owe you by the end of the month."

"No, that's okay." Cara would have accepted but she knew Marcy had financial struggles of her own. "As long as the boss at my day job pays me on time, I should be fine."

A nervous chuckle escaped Marcy's throat. "Something isn't right with that situation. I've never heard of a company paying late and getting away with it for so long."

Cara sighed. "Trust me, I know. But I need that job. I can't exactly afford to ask questions."

"I heard one of the offices we clean might have an opening soon. I'll keep my ears open for you."

"Thanks."

"So, what's this about a tall, dark, Latin stud paying you a visit yesterday?"

Cara's eyes flew open and she sat up straight. "What? Did Mom tell you about that?"

Marcy giggled. "Yeah, when I picked you up this evening. Said he dropped by the house driving a car so fancy she'd never heard of it before."

"Oh geez. It was nothing."

Marcy's eyebrow lifted. "Oh really? She said he paid you and Isaac a visit at the hospital yesterday. When were you planning on telling me about this?"

"Darn it!" Cara groaned. "It's nothing. He felt bad because his girlfriend got me fired."

"Oh really?" Marcy was suddenly disappointed. "So he has a girlfriend?"

"Well, he says she's not but they were sitting together." Cara huffed. "It was one of those snobby fundraisers on the upper east side. I sure as heck won't miss those."

"So, she's not his girlfriend?" There was a glimmer of hope in

Marcy's tone.

"I see where you're going with this and I don't have the energy for it right now."

"Oh, come on, Cara. He went to your house and then tracked you down at the hospital. This is huge. I can't believe you weren't even gonna mention it."

"I told you, there's nothing to mention. He's a rich guy who obviously has too much time on his hands and guilt issues of some sort."

"So? What kind of guy drives from Manhattan to Newark because of a woman he's just met? Sounds like a dream to me."

"Like I said, he has too much time on his hands. He was probably bored from sitting around and counting his money all day."

"Oh, you are so frustrating." Marcy took her eyes from the road to gape at Cara for a moment. "He could've just had some money sent to you. Or had a gift sent to the hospital or whatever." She could barely see Cara's face in the dark, but she thought she noticed a smirk when she mentioned a gift. "What? Did he send you a gift? Bring you one in person?"

Cara growled and stared up at the ceiling. "He brought Isaac a gift."

Marcy gasped. "What was it?"

"It was nothing."

"Bullshit! What the heck did he bring Isaac at the hospital?"

"A care package." Cara's voice grew quiet. "A very nice care package."

"Aw." Marcy pouted. "I wish I had a rich man to bring me a care package." She chuckled. "I wonder if there's another package he'd rather give you instead—"

Cara laughed. "Stop! I can't let myself think that way about him."

"What? Maybe you should call him and see what happens. You could use a good romp in the bedroom. How long's it been now? Let me think…you moved back here six months ago…it had to be when you were living in Chicago…"

"Stop. Please." Cara tried to stifle her groan. "It's too depressing to think about. Besides, you should see the woman he was with. Perfect in every way."

"Probably surgically enhanced."

Cara shrugged. "Yeah, maybe. But what's it matter? I mean, look at me? I'd have a better shot with George the forklift operator who comes to the office just to wink at me every chance he gets."

Marcy slapped Cara's leg. "None of that talk. If you want, we can start working out before or after work. That office building on Claremont has a gym they'd probably let us use."

"No way. I'm too tired from working all day then cleaning offices with you every night. No time."

"Well, suit yourself. I think you should give the hot rich man a go. Your mom said he gave you his card and told you to," she slowed her words, "call anytime."

"Yeah, yeah."

Marcy made her voice deliberately sensual. "Yes, anytime. About anything you need. Hello, Mr. Manhattan Heartthrob? Think you could spare an evening to give my friend here some personal attention? It's been so long—"

"Stop!" Cara's head shook. "Why does your mind always go there? He was a nice guy. A gentleman." She paused to sigh. "And he could have any woman he wants. I'm sure he keeps a whole slew of girls around to fill those needs. Rich guy with a sports car. Yeah." She snorted. "He has to drive all the way to Newark to get laid. That's believable."

"Maybe he doesn't *need* to come to Newark. Maybe he just wanted to. Maybe you made an impression."

"Please, don't." Cara closed her mouth to keep the words, "I don't want to get my hopes up," from coming out.

"Okay. Well, no matter what, you need to start making time for yourself. You do so much for everyone else. We all just wanna see you happy."

"I *am* happy."

"You'd be happier if you'd let handsome men be nice to you instead of running them off. He gave you his card. You should give him a call."

"Between Isaac and work, when do I have time for that? I'm worn out in every way."

"Hmm. You don't sound too happy to me."

"Okay, whatever. Maybe I don't have time for happy. Can we drop it now?"

* * *

"What the heck?" Cara stared in disbelief at the chains around the door at Doyle Construction. She pulled on the handle, trying to get inside. The heavy chain rattled, but the door was locked tight. "What in the world is this?" She squinted to look through the glass door. "Mr. Doyle? You in there? You all right?"

With her heels digging against the sidewalk, she tried again to pull the door open. Again, the chains rattled.

She reached inside her purse for her phone just as two men in suits walked around the corner, meeting her at the front door.

"You work here?" One of the men asked.

"Uh…" She stammered.

"It's okay. Don't be nervous. You're not in trouble. Do you work here?"

She looked him in the eye. "Yes."

The other guy snorted. "You don't anymore. This is an IRS seizure."

Cara gasped. "What do you mean, I don't work here anymore?"

"Your boss owes the IRS a hefty sum in payroll taxes, ma'am."

"Oh my God." She looked down at the chains. "So I can't go back in there? At all?"

"Nope. If you got some personal stuff in your desk in there we can probably talk about it but, for all intents and purposes, this business is shut down." He smirked. "Did you ever wonder why he paid you in cash?"

"Um…yeah. Was that not allowed?" she asked.

The guys shared a look then turned to her. One answered, "It's not ideal. He thought he was getting away with paying you under the table. Did he issue check stubs that showed your withholding?"

Cara nodded. "Yes. Once a month or so he'd give us all a statement. I thought it was legit. Am I in trouble?"

"No. Doyle's in trouble."

Her eyes welled up. "But he was supposed to pay me tomorrow. What am I gonna do?"

"He'll undergo a full-scale audit and we'll figure out what he owes us and what he owes his employees." He frowned. "I hate to tell you, ma'am, but the audit'll take a while and even then, you may never see that money. I'm sorry. It's always the employees who get hurt the most in these situations."

"Okay," Cara said. If the IRS agents told her anything else, she was too numb with anger and worry to hear it. She simply walked to her car and drove out of the parking lot, unsure what she was going to do next.

When she got home, she yelled, "I'm back!" to her mom in

the kitchen, then went right upstairs to Isaac's room where he lay in bed. His tired eyes perked up when he saw her.

"Mommy!" His voice was scratchy. He reached out for her with both arms. "Mommy Mommy Mommy!"

Her heart melted at the sight of his smile. She dropped her purse to the floor and sat down on the bed beside him for a quick hug. "You croak like a frog when you talk." She pulled away, smiling and ruffling his shaggy blond hair with her fingers. "You're Mommy's little croaky frog."

He laughed. "I'm not a cwoaky fwog."

"Yes you are." She leaned down to kiss his cheek. "Did you have your popsicle after I left this morning?"

"Yes. And some gwape Jeh-wo."

"Good."

"Can we go to the pawk now?"

"No, baby. You need to get some rest."

"But aw I do is west." His eyes got big. "I need to see Joey. He was s'posed to bwing me a wace caw."

"Joey and the race car can wait, sweetie. I know you feel a lot better but you'll get sick again if you go outside to play too soon."

His little lips formed a frown. "No I won't."

"Yes you will. You don't wanna go back to the hospital, do you?"

"No."

"Okay then. You stay here in bed. If you feel good later, maybe we can walk outside for a minute. But we need to make sure you get better so you can go back to the park and see your friends again."

"Gwammah said my tonsahs a gwow back if I weave bed for too wong."

Cara didn't know how to answer. She despised the idea of

lying to her son, and she didn't know Patty had concocted this idea. But she also didn't like the idea of him not getting enough rest after surgery. "Well, if you thought your tonsils would grow back, why'd you wanna go to the park?"

"I want a wace caw." He grinned.

Patty appeared at the door. "What are you doing home so soon? What happened? Why didn't you call?"

"Shh." Cara's eyes widened at her mom. She turned back to Isaac. "I'm gonna go get you some more to drink. We'll talk about that race car later." Cara stood and turned on the small television to Isaac's favorite cartoon channel, then left the room.

"So?" Patty asked, her hand on her hip. She followed her daughter downstairs. "What happened?"

Cara raced down to the kitchen, trying to put this talk off as long as possible. Like she could change the past if she didn't talk about it. "I lost my job."

"What?" Patty brought her hand to her chest. "You got fired?"

"Not exactly." Cara opened the refrigerator and took out a small bottle of apple juice. When she plunked it down on the kitchen table, tears ran down her face. "They shut the company down."

"Who shut the company down?"

"The IRS." She sniffled. "Doyle owed taxes." Her cry changed to a high-pitched wail. "I'll probably never get the money they owe me."

Patty put her arms around her daughter and let her cry against her shoulder.

Cara continued through her tears. "What am I gonna do? I've applied for jobs everywhere. There's nothing."

"We'll see if you can get some unemployment." She rubbed her back. "And you can stay here and help me fill some cake orders."

Cara groaned at that thought. Her mom worked at a bakery before she retired. She now lived on a fixed income and baked for the few cake orders she received. Cara, however, hated to cook. She felt she just wasn't born with that gene, and her mom's skills had never rubbed off on her. "If you get a lot of orders I'll help, I guess."

"Don't worry, dear. We'll be okay. You make enough from Marcy's cleaning service to pay for groceries for you and Isaac. We'll scrape by."

Cara pulled away from her, wiping her face with her hands. "I don't want to just 'scrape by,' Mom. I was trying to save money so I could relocate when I finally get another job offer."

"I know that, but life doesn't always go the way we want."

Cara scoffed. "You don't have to tell me that. I learn that lesson, daily."

Patty rubbed Cara's shoulder. "You know, I think you're missing the obvious here."

"What's that?"

Patty sighed wistfully. "A certain rich Mexican gentleman who gave you his business card—"

"Oh, Mom." She shook her head. "Will you stop talking about that? I know you told Marcy all about it, too. Look, he's probably moved on to some other charity case by now. Just because he's rich, it doesn't mean he's sane." She picked up the juice bottle and started toward the stairs. "Trust me, he's gotta be crazy to come all the way out here like he did. Remember that movie we saw about that girl who fell in love with that oil tycoon and he was psycho and killed her whole family?"

"That was a *Lifetime* movie. It wasn't real."

"Oh, I'm pretty sure it was based on actual events." Cara knew it was a stretch but she had grown tired of her mom's nagging. "Think about it. A guy like that could ruin our lives.

He might be a total nut job."

"Sure, he might be. Or he might *not* be. Seemed like a nice guy as far as I could tell. Very down to Earth. And he loved my cooking."

Cara sighed as she walked upstairs. "Everyone loves your cooking. Especially psychos."

"I don't care what you say. If you don't call him, I will."

Cara shook her head. As she approached Isaac's room, she thought she heard him talking aloud, maybe to the television. But her mouth dropped open when she saw him laughing with her cell phone to his ear.

"Uh-huh," Isaac said into the phone, laughing hysterically. "Cwoaky fwog."

Cara ran across the room. "Who are you talking to?"

He put both hands on the phone, holding it like he didn't want to let it go. "Bictow."

"Big toe?" Cara snatched the phone and brought it to her ear. "Who's this?"

A man laughed. "*Big toe.*" He laughed some more. "*I mean, Victor.*" He cleared his throat. "*Victor Barboza.*"

Her eyes and mouth both dropped open. She stared at Patty as she rushed to the hallway for privacy. She stumbled over her words, nervous. "Um…um…my son isn't supposed to be using my cell phone. I'm sorry."

"*Don't be sorry. I'm the one who called him. Smart little guy.*" Victor paused. "*So, I hear you might be in need of new employment.*"

Oh Lord, he really is *psycho*, she thought. How did he know that already? Had he planted a microphone in the house? "Uh…I don't know what to say."

"*Say you'll come to my office to interview for a position. It's in public relations. We could use someone with your experience.*"

"How do you know anything about my experience?"

"*Found your resume online.*"

"Oh."

"*Says here you ran some national projects. Very impressive. Too bad the company's doing so poorly or they'd probably rehire you. Anyway, be here this afternoon. Two o'clock. I'll email you with directions.*"

"Well, uh…sure, I guess."

"*Good. See you then.*" Victor hung up.

Perplexed, Cara stared down at the phone in her hand. "How did he get my number?" In a huff, she walked into Isaac's room where her mom was watching him drink juice, a big smile plastered across her face. "Mother, dear," Cara often used this term for her mother when she was upset, "do you know how Mr. Barboza got my phone number? Because it sure wasn't from me."

Patty set her smile on Isaac as she said in a singsong tone, "I don't know, I may have given it to him when he stopped by a few days ago."

"Mom!"

"What? He asked for it. And he was so polite."

Cara paced the floor. "Well, he already found out, somehow, that I lost my job."

Patty's eyes met Cara's. "What?"

"Yeah. How did he know that? I didn't put my new phone number or Doyle Construction on my online resume. He wants me to interview for a job at two o'clock today." She lowered her voice and leaned in closer, covering most of her mouth so Isaac couldn't see. She whispered, "*Psycho!*"

Patty's lips formed a thin line. She spoke quietly, her mouth barely moving, "You need a job, don't you?"

"Yeah, but not like this."

Patty's eyes rolled. "You better go pick out what you're gonna wear to that interview."

Cara groaned. "Oh…" she paused, looking at Isaac as she stopped herself from saying "shit." She hit her forehead with her palm. "I hope something fits. It's been so long since I had to wear one of my nice suits."

"You'll be fine. You have time to go shopping. I'm sure the mall has plenty of clearance racks this time of year."

Isaac's eyes lit up. "The maw?"

Patty shook her head, angry with herself for using one of their forbidden words. "Not today. Maybe next week."

Isaac pouted. "No maw?" His expression quickly changed to a smile. "What about the pawk? Mommy said I could go."

"No," Cara said. "I'm right here and I said you could go outside for a minute. Not to the park."

Isaac's smile disappeared. "Can Bictow take me to the pawk?"

Patty laughed.

Cara answered. "No, baby. Drink your juice and you'll be back at the park in no time." She kissed his cheek, then turned around and left the room, ignoring her mother's snide grin.

CHAPTER FOUR

Victor smiled at the clock. It was one-thirty. Cara had replied to his email with a simple, "Thank you. See you at two."

He sensed her hesitation and he tried to see it her way. Maybe it was strange that he was so forward, inviting her to an interview, knowing she'd lost her job that morning. But she needed his help and he felt justified in his actions. After all, Doyle Construction was already under scrutiny of the IRS. All Victor did was call in a favor to speed up the process. Soon, she'd have a better job in a nicer environment. That's all that mattered.

He went over her resume again for at least the twentieth time. Thankfully, a lot of people owed him favors or he'd never get anyone to make room in the budget for a new employee, especially someone in public relations. It was one of the few areas that had to make cutbacks. He pored over her skills and experience, trying to think of a brand new position he could create just for her. Something that would overlap to his division. Then he let out a soft chuckle. Hiring Cara was a done deal. He could always think of reasons to borrow an employee. Why was he stressing about it so much? He'd keep her duties vague for now until he really found something for her to do.

The woman had some kind of hold on him. It was undeniable. His heart raced every time he thought about her. The sound of her melodic voice on the phone drove him wild. She was a breath of fresh air in his life. Fresh air he didn't know his life was missing.

The phone on his desk buzzed at fifteen minutes till two.

"Yes?" he answered.

Gary said, "*Ms. Green's here for her two o'clock.*"

He swallowed, tempering his voice in case she could hear. "Thanks. Please ask her to have a seat in the waiting area. I'm almost ready."

Victor stood and walked to the sideboard, straightening his tie in the mirror on the wall above it. He had to calm down and act like he was really interviewing her. Like he hadn't invented a fictitious job posting to spend time with her. He made sure he had a list of questions to ask, printed straight off the Internet. Screening new employees wasn't one of his usual duties. The last person he'd interviewed was his assistant, Gary, and that was almost an entire year earlier.

He flattened his palms, sliding them against his suit to make sure they weren't sweating. He hadn't been this nervous about a woman in years. As he rushed around his desk to his chair, he pushed a button on his desk phone. "You may show her in now."

When the door opened, Victor stood behind his desk, waiting and watching. Cara's long blond hair floated across her shoulders as she turned around to smile and say, "Thank you," to Gary, who held the door.

Cara then looked straight ahead at Victor and said, "Hi," before her eyes went around the room, bouncing among the furnishings. The door closed softly behind her. "Nice, big office you have here. I've never seen anything like it."

"It's a perk of being one of the partners." Victor grinned. "We always get the best stuff."

"Oh, I didn't realize you were a partner. Your title is 'Chief Consultant,' right?" She now stood in front of his desk, clutching her briefcase against her stomach.

He gulped as he peered into her shimmering green eyes. "Yes. But it's just a worthless moniker. I made it up myself. I stay out of the day-to-day operations and try to keep a low profile." He gestured for her to have a seat.

She nodded and smoothed the back of her black skirt before sitting.

He waited until she was in her chair before he sat. Then he clenched his teeth, feeling like an idiot. He had forgotten to shake her hand. That would certainly tip her off to the informality of this interview. Nonchalantly, he slid his hand across his pants and rose slightly in his chair. "How rude of me. I didn't shake your hand."

She followed his lead and stood up just enough to lean forward, reaching across the desk. "I guess that's the proper job interview protocol, right?"

Victor smiled and kept his eyes on hers as they exchanged a firm handshake. Unfortunately, she had bent forward enough to barely show her full breasts peeking out atop her tight blouse.

As she eased back down in her seat, her hand went to her blouse's top button, tugging it up toward her neck.

Shit, she caught me looking, he thought. *Time for a quick subject change.* "So, Ms. Green," he said, "I'm glad you were able to meet with me on such short notice."

She shrugged, then pulled a notebook and pen out of her briefcase. "It's not like I had anywhere else to be. You knew that, Mr. Barboza." She smirked. "Would you mind telling me how you knew about Doyle Construction?"

"I knew where you worked because your mother mentioned it when we spoke."

"Yes, but how'd you know they were shut down this morning?"

He half-smiled and folded his hands on the desk in front of him. "Coincidence, I guess. New York is a big city but it's still a small world. You'd be surprised how many people I know around here." Before she could speak again, he picked up her resume and continued. "So, you've worked for two companies since graduating college. One of them Fortune 500."

"Yes."

"Which company was your favorite?"

"Lowdon and Shore, definitely. They promoted from within and offered a wonderful benefits package. I would have stayed there if they hadn't cut most of my department. I hoped to stay till retirement."

"That's good to hear." Victor stared at the resume, thankful he'd made notes in the margins to remind him of what to ask. Otherwise, the excitement he felt from seeing her right in front of him would have caused his mind to go completely blank. "We're looking for employees who wish to stay with us for the long haul. And we offer excellent benefits as well, to ensure we keep our best people." He put the paper down and looked at her. "Are you planning a move back to Chicago, or would you like to stay in the area?"

"If I can find a decent job here, I'll gladly stay."

"Great."

Her eyebrows lifted. "If you don't mind, could you tell me more about the position I'm being considered for? I couldn't find any job listings on your company website."

"Yes." He breathed deeply, trying to remember the vague job

description that he now realized he should have written down. "It'll be called Public Relations Liaison. You'll work with each division as needed to help us streamline our overall business marketing plan."

"Who would I report to?"

He glanced down at her resume. "This office. So, do you have any experience in finance at all?"

"You mean, I'd report directly to you?"

"Yes."

"I've never heard of a job like this before. The duties sound awfully vague."

"They'll firm up as we go. It's one of our newer positions. Like most companies, we have openings we don't advertise because we wait till we meet the right people to fill them. It usually happens through networking."

"But you don't know me at all, yet somehow you think I'm the right person for the job because your girlfriend got me fired the other night?" Cara crossed her legs.

Victor inhaled a rush of air, his heart pounding a fierce new rhythm. Her dark skirt ended just above her knee and contrasted perfectly with her light, silky skin. Her legs looked completely bare, like she wasn't wearing pantyhose. He imagined sliding his hand along her thigh to see if her skin was as soft as it looked.

After a few seconds she began pulling at the hem of her skirt, trying to cover her knee.

Victor felt his cheeks flush; she'd obviously caught him staring. He cleared his throat and decided not to draw attention. "I'm sorry, what was your question?"

Cara swept a lock of her blond hair onto her back. Her cheeks were getting red as well. "I was just asking what made you think I'm the right person for this job? You don't even know me. Is it because your girlfriend got me fired the other night? Are you *that* motivated by guilt?"

Victor's jaw almost dropped, but he caught himself and began to chuckle instead of getting angry. He should kick her out of his office for her snarky attitude about his generous offer. But he quickly remembered what her mother told him about her independence. Cara was the type of woman who'd rather live on the street than find herself beholden to a man. He was now seeing it for himself, and it only piqued his interest even more. "First off, that woman is not my girlfriend. And second, this isn't about guilt. I can read people pretty well from a first impression and I can tell you're a hard worker and a fighter. Exactly the kind of person this company needs." He cocked his head to the side. "And by the way, I called your references, the ones I found on the second page of your resume. The only bad quality anyone mentioned was your stubbornness." The part about her being stubborn was the only thing he made up, but he wanted to see if she'd squirm.

Cara's lips pursed in defiance. "So, there really is a job and you're not just some rich psychopath who's decided to stalk my family for no reason?" She uncrossed her legs and brought her knees close together, but folded her arms over her chest.

Before he could respond to her question, his eyes went to her cleavage, which was now more prominent with the way she was sitting. Her tight beige blouse peeked out from under her black blazer, the material straining against those full mounds. He looked into her eyes, hoping he'd stopped before making an ass out of himself this time. "Yes, there's really a job. And it's yours." He smirked, making sure his voice oozed sarcasm. "That is, unless you have another high-level receptionist job lined up at another shady construction company. I'd hate to take you away from that."

Cara narrowed her gaze at him, her tone slightly subdued. "No, I have nothing else lined up."

"So you'll take the job then?"

Cara's eyes rolled. "There's something weird about this. You must have an angle. This is all a little too…convenient."

Victor shrugged. "Sometimes things are convenient. Life doesn't always have to be so hard."

"Strangers aren't this nice to each other for no reason."

Victor sat up straight, then leaned forward for emphasis. *Why is she so resistant?* His gut feeling told him there was something more than a stubborn personality, but his only concern right now was getting her to say she'd take the job. This sexy, luscious woman had captured his attention like no woman had in years. "Don't worry about my reasons. Just do the right thing for your family." Hastily, he took a pen and scribbled on a nearby notepad. "I'm writing down a number. You tell me if this annual salary is acceptable to you." When he finished, he shoved the paper across the desk.

Cara's eyes grew wide when she saw the figure. It was almost double what she made in Chicago. "I don't know if I can live up to this. I'm pretty sure the head of my department didn't even make this much money at my last job."

"Cost of living. It's much higher here than Chicago. Come on. We can use someone with your skills."

"The cost of living isn't *that* much higher here."

He put his hands on his desk, fingers laced together. "In these situations you're supposed to negotiate a higher salary, not a lower one."

"I guess I'm not like most people."

"No, you're not. That's why I need to hire you. Come on. Say you'll work for me."

She leaned forward in her chair, staring at the scrap of paper atop his desk. Her voice was weak. "Yes. I'll work for you. I'll do my best to live up to your high expectations."

"Great." He displayed a grin, not the beaming smile he hid inside. "You can start on Monday.

"Monday? I can start tomorrow morning if you'd like."

"No. Please take the rest of the week to care for your son." Victor smiled. "And tell him Big Toe says hi."

Cara blushed at the remembrance of his conversation with her son. She nervously bit her bottom lip. "That's it? We're finished with the interview?"

His jaw firmly set, he confidently said, "Yes, that's it." He knew he should have kept the interview going a little longer but she'd caught him off guard with her own line of questions. "Oh, and here." He pulled an envelope out of his top drawer and handed it to her. "It's a small advance. It'll be withheld from your upcoming paychecks at a rate you can determine when you fill out your new hire paperwork." His friend at the IRS had informed him that most of the employees at Doyle Construction had not been paid in a while.

She peeked inside the envelope and let out a tiny gasp. "Are you sure? Is this because you feel bad about—"

"Ms. Green, if we're going to have a good working relationship, you're going to have to stop asking so many questions about how I do business. Your job will be to streamline our public relations. Employee benefits are determined elsewhere."

"Okay…if you're sure about this."

"Absolutely." He turned to his computer, typing. "I'm sending an email to HR. Take the elevator down to the third floor and follow the signs to the main HR reception area. They'll get you all set up." He finished typing and stood. "Now, let me show you out and I'll see you Monday."

They both walked to the door. Cara said, "Thank you again," and reached down to turn the knob at the same time as Victor. When his hand covered hers, she inhaled a gasp in embarrassment, expecting him to move.

But Victor's eyes caught hers. His hand lingered for a moment before he took it away. "See you Monday."

He was still looking into her eyes when she opened the door to leave.

* * *

Marcy and Patty bombarded Cara the instant she walked through the door.

Marcy yelped in excitement and took the giant Macy's bag full of clearance rack clothes from Cara's arm. "Tell me everything! Tell me everything!"

Patty took her daughter's wrist and pulled her into the living room. "Yes! Don't leave out a thing."

Cara unbuttoned her blazer and kicked off her shoes. "Where's Isaac?"

"Don't worry," Patty said. "I finally got him to take a nap a few minutes ago. He's fine. Come on. What happened?"

Marcy sat on the couch, dumping the contents of the bag beside her. "Holy cow! The new job must be upscale. Look at these."

Cara, in a daze, shook her head and took a seat on the opposite side of her new pile of clothes. "No, they were all on sale."

Patty sat in the recliner, her eyes huge behind her wide-rimmed glasses. "So, out with it. Tell us all about your big day."

Marcy and Patty both looked at Cara, who was now staring straight ahead at nothing, wondering where to start.

Cara took another moment to think, then put her hand on her chest, over her top button. She let out a sigh of relief. "Oh good. It held. I'm about to bust out of this top. Thank God for safety pins." She stuck her palms against her eyes, whining. "Oh shit, I think he noticed, too. He thinks I'm too poor to buy clothes. That's why he gave me a check today."

"What?" Patty asked. "He gave you money?"

"Yes," Cara said. "He thinks I'm pathetic. It's an advance on my paycheck. That's how I bought all these new clothes today. I barely have any nice clothes in my closet that fit anymore. I could wear anything to Doyle and they didn't care."

Marcy picked up a long blue skirt, inspecting it from top to bottom. "But he didn't know that, did he?"

Patty said, "Yeah, you didn't tell him you needed money, did you?"

"No." Cara's eyes rolled. "He seems to know a lot more about me than he should." She glared at Patty. "Have you been keeping in touch with him since you met him the other day? Did you tell him Doyle owes me money?"

"Absolutely not, hon," Patty said. "I think he does his research because he likes you."

Cara sighed. "No, he doesn't. I promise. You should've seen the way he looked at me today. I'm a charity case to him." She let out a loud groan. "Would you believe I ripped a huge hole in my pantyhose when I got out of the car? I had to take 'em off. He kept staring at my legs." She huffed. "Probably at my varicose veins. I was so embarrassed. But at least I remembered to shave."

Marcy snickered and shot a funny look at Patty. "Are you hearing what I'm hearing? Sounds to me like he was checking her out."

Patty nodded. "Yes, I was just thinking the same thing. He was looking at your legs."

"Ugh," Cara said. "Why would he do that? I felt like a stuffed sausage in this outfit. I should've worn my body shaper to keep everything in place." In her heart, even with the extra weight, Cara didn't feel unattractive. She always turned a few approving heads when she went out in public. But she was afraid to get her hopes up about Victor.

"I don't know why you're so down on yourself," Marcy said. "You're as pretty as ever."

Cara picked up a blouse from the pile. "I'm not pretty enough to land a guy like Victor. And I'm not sure I'd even want to. He seems like a control freak."

Patty slapped her own knee as she laughed. "God help the man who ever tries to control you."

Patty and Marcy shared a long laugh at Cara's expense.

Determined not to let them get to her, Cara stood up and headed to the stairs. "I don't care what you guys think. It's stupid to think a guy like Victor Barboza would ever be interested in someone like me. You should've seen that woman he was with at the charity dinner."

Patty shook her head. "You don't give yourself enough credit. The guy's obviously interested. Just let it happen and stop being so *you* about it."

Marcy gasped and brought her hand to her mouth. "It's like a fairy tale come true. Cara, you deserve a fairy tale. Don't chase him away."

Cara let out a frustrated growl. "Fairy tales do *not* come true. You've been watching too many movies. Or reading too many of those cheesy romance novels about regular girls getting swept away by the dashing billionaire." She sighed as she walked upstairs, her voice trailing off. "What a load of crap."

CHAPTER FIVE

It was eleven-thirty on Cara's first day at Monarch Enterprises, and so far it was uneventful. She had spent most of the morning sitting through employee safety videos that would probably never apply to her. Gary, Victor's assistant, had given her the grand tour of the building.

But there had been no sign of Victor.

And in a way, Cara was grateful. She'd spent hours on Sunday trying on outfits, determining the ones that were most flattering. After her embarrassing display at the interview, she wanted to prove she was a polished professional. Victor's absence this morning at least gave her a reprieve from that anxiety.

At the same time, where was he? If she had allowed herself to think he actually liked her—which she strived *not* to do— she may have been offended that he didn't make time to see her on her first day. It meant she was right all along. This job was an act of pity, and nothing more.

I told you so, she said to herself.

And for once, she wished she hadn't been right. Unfortunately, there was a shred of hope within her that allowed her to entertain fantasies of the tall, dark, handsome dream man. A man who was so far out of her league, he wasn't even in her universe. Surely he spent his weekends chasing young, flighty debutantes who were barely legal. The sort of women who were bred to be trophy wives. That life definitely wasn't for her. It was Cara and Isaac against the world. Maybe soon she'd have enough money saved to move them into a nice apartment in the city and send him to a good pre-school. That's all that mattered.

Bored with filling out yet another set of new hire paperwork, Cara went to the break room Gary had shown her earlier. If she didn't have any real work to do yet, at least she could figure out how to use the space age-looking digital coffee machine.

As she took a small paper cup from the counter, a woman in a blue dress entered the room. She had sandy brown hair and looked to be in her late twenties, about Cara's age. She gave Cara a smile and said, "I don't think we've met. Are you new here?"

"Yes, I'm new. My name's Cara Green."

"Rhonda Flint. Mr. Noonan's assistant. Nice to meet you." Rhonda opened the refrigerator door. "So, you the new assistant, here in acquisitions?"

"Um…no?" Cara stopped to consider the question. She knew so little about her new job, she had no idea if Victor's department was casually referred to as "acquisitions." "I report to Mr. Barboza. My title is Public Relations Liaison."

Rhonda abruptly closed the refrigerator door and gave her a wide-eyed glance. "What?"

Oh no. "Is that a bad thing?"

Rhonda's high heels clopped along the floor as she walked up to Cara. She looked over her shoulder as if someone were eavesdropping. "You might not wanna talk about that too loudly. Barboza doesn't hire people. The whole company's under a pretty tight hiring freeze unless it's urgent."

"So, what do I tell people if they ask?" Cara chuckled. "I can't exactly lie and say I'm somewhere else."

"Hmm. That's true." Rhonda's lips puckered as she thought about it. "I know. You tell 'em you're a consultant, working on a project for Barboza. And if anyone asks about the project, you tell 'em you can't talk about it.

"Okay." Cara was skeptical.

"Gary." Rhonda simultaneously rolled her eyes and blew her bangs out of her face. "He should've warned you." She smirked. "He's gay, you know."

Cara nodded. "Yeah, I got that." She'd noticed some pictures on Gary's screen saver that morning of him with another man in a position that was slightly more than friendly. But then she had a thought. "Oh wait, you mean Gary, not Mr. Barboza, right?"

Rhonda tossed her head back, laughing hard. "Yes, Gary. Barboza…hell no."

Cara didn't like the sound of that. "What do you mean?"

Rhonda stopped laughing. "Oh, nothing. Your boss is the most eligible bachelor in the building. Hell, in the whole city. At least he is now. He was engaged for a long time." Rhonda cleared her throat and changed the subject, her eyes flickering as if she knew she shouldn't be confiding so much gossip in the new girl. "So anyway, Gary probably should've told you to keep your new job a little private around here. We just had lunch last week. Wonder why he didn't tell me there was a new hire?"

"What's the big deal? People come and go all the time."

"That's not it. People don't come and go in Barboza's group. It's just him and Gary."

"Is that strange?"

"For this place, yeah. He's the only partner who doesn't oversee a whole staff. All we know is, he knows his shit and he brings in a lot of business." Her eyes were huge. "And we don't know anything else."

Cara gasped, thinking about the unsavory owner of Doyle Construction, where she sensed all along that something wasn't right. "Is he doing something illegal? Please tell me he's not."

"Oh no. Nothing like that. He's a good guy. Keeps to himself." She shrugged. "And really friendly when you see him around." Her voice got quiet. "But I hear he's a playboy."

Cara's heart sank. "Really? Is that why he's single?"

Rhonda's brow arched and she looked around the room, suddenly feeling the urge to confide a piece of juicy gossip in the new girl. "You can't repeat this. Hell, you could find it online if you knew where to look. But there's a rumor his engagement ended because of infidelity. We all think he cheated with a girl who got fired the week before it happened."

"Oh no!"

"Yes. Of course, it's just a rumor, but still." Rhonda sighed. "So, tell me a little about you. New to the area? Married? Kids?"

"I'm from Newark originally but I just moved back home after losing my job in Chicago. This is my first real job in months. Never been married. One kid, Isaac. He's three."

Rhonda grinned. "I got a three-year-old, too. A girl, Justine. Also got a five-year-old, Aidan. And I got a no-good cheatin' ex-husband. The divorce was final last month."

"Oh, I'm so sorry."

"It's okay. Could be worse. Could've had that third kid we were trying for when I found those pictures on his cell phone. What about you? You got a cheatin' man, too?"

"No." Cara nervously straightened the cuff of her sleeve. The situation with Isaac's dad was a secret she'd decided long ago to take with her to the grave. It was easier to tell everyone she never knew his dad than to tell them the truth. "Isaac was my gift from a one-night stand my last semester in college. Never saw him again. I consider my son to be my graduation present." She smiled.

"Ah. Well, you're better off anyway." Rhonda looked at her watch. "I gotta get back to my desk but I'll come over for some chitchat later if you like. They give you an office or a cubicle?"

"An office." Cara swallowed, hard. After this conversation, she was reluctant to mention she'd been given a spacious office with a spectacular view.

"Okay. I'll come over there and find you later." Rhonda patted Cara's shoulder. "Take care. Nice meeting you."

Cara waited until Rhonda was safely out of the break room before leaving herself. It was good to make a friend at her new job so soon, but with Victor keeping such a low profile, she wasn't sure it was smart to hang out with one of the office gossips so quickly.

No matter. With her head held high, she left the break room and went back to her office, trying not to obsess about this new information she'd received about her boss. Was he really a playboy? Did he cheat on his fiancee? Is that who he was with the night they met? It would make sense and possibly explain why that lady was so furious about him talking to another woman in front of her.

Cara had to get herself to stop thinking about it. After all, he was just her boss and this was simply her work place. Nothing more. What he did in his personal life was none of her business.

She took a deep breath with the realization that she definitely had a crush on him. And that sucked.

* * *

"Damn it!" Victor was almost angry enough to curse aloud in Spanish today.

If it wasn't one thing, it was another. A meeting ran too long. Then a traffic jam. An important business associate needed an hour-long phone call to make a simple decision. And now, another traffic jam. He had looked forward to this morning for days, and it seemed like fate was working against him. But he would not be discouraged.

All morning, his thoughts were with Cara. Was she happy in her new job so far? Had Gary made her feel comfortable in the office?

Was there any chance at all that she had been thinking about him the way he was thinking about her?

His interest in Cara had grown immensely since he'd last seen her, made worse by the fact that he'd done some informal detective work…via Facebook. She only had five pictures available for public view and he could've probably found a way to see them all, but it made him feel creepy. *Successful businessmen don't cyber stalk, do they?* He chuckled to himself. It didn't matter what others did. He had to find a way to see her and he was grateful for the pictures.

There were, however, no public pictures of Isaac. Victor could still hear his high-pitched voice on the phone, mispronouncing words. So cute. He had never thought of dating a woman who had a child before, but now, he wanted to.

Victor wasn't much older than Isaac when his own father passed away but some of those early memories stuck with him in tiny fragments. The most vivid memories were of the way he laughed when he and his brothers climbed all over him like they were wrestling. His father always pretended he was losing, and the brothers always reveled in their victory. They had no idea how poor they were; a family of five living in a tiny clay house with no running water and barely enough food to eat. But Victor was grateful for those hard times. He knew they helped mold him into the man he was today.

As he sat in a long line of cars at a busy intersection, he took a moment to analyze his obsession with Cara once again. Perhaps she'd merely come along at a time when he needed someone like her. A real woman. A woman of substance, in every way, her life somehow crashing into his and bringing back memories he'd buried long ago. She was unlike any woman he'd met in a very long time. Hell, maybe ever.

He took out his phone and looked at one of the pictures he'd found online. Wisps of blond hair framed her face so perfectly. *God, she's beautiful.* How he wanted to taste those plump lips. Mmm. And peel her out of that dress…

Victor took a deep breath and put his phone away. He couldn't let himself think about it right now. Soon, he'd see her and welcome her to the office. What if she was still way too rebellious and skeptical of his motives? Shit. She had every reason to be. That was another reason why he absolutely must act professionally around her.

He ignored his urge to buy her flowers to welcome her aboard. It took him approximately five minutes to realize what a stupid, dead giveaway that would be. Damn it, the woman made him think irrationally, and he found that extremely frustrating.

Women were never this much of a challenge to him.

Several minutes passed and he finally entered the parking garage. Quickly, he parked and took the elevator to the top floor. As he stepped out of it, he adjusted his tie and his jacket, then headed around the corner, stopping at Gary's desk.

"Nice to see you, Mr. Barboza. Long morning?" Gary swiveled in his chair, smiling.

Victor's head shook. "You don't wanna know." He grabbed an unopened letter on the counter in front of Gary's desk, pausing for a second so he didn't sound too excited about the question on his mind. Then he stared mindlessly at the envelope and asked, "So, is our new employee having a good first day?"

Gary leaned forward as if listening for a distant sound. "You can ask her yourself if you like. That sounds like her now."

Victor's heart raced as he turned his head frantically in the direction of the footsteps and unconsciously adjusted his tie again.

And there she was, the lovely blonde of his fantasies, wearing a pin-striped navy blue suit that looked like it was made to set off her best assets.

Her eyes met his for a split second, then she glanced down at the floor with a slight grin.

Does she have any idea what she does to me?

He stood still, waiting for her to walk up to him, but she shyly stopped a few feet away. *She's a walking contradiction.* During their short interview she was all guts. Today, she was timid, but that was good. It gave him the upper hand. Suddenly, he didn't feel so nervous.

Victor calmly extended his hand. "Ms. Green. Welcome."

She took one step closer and slowly put her hand around his. "Mr. Barboza. Thank you for having me."

*Her skin's like velvet…*His breath hitched as her fingers lightly grazed the inside of his wrist. *Shit, now isn't the time…*

He pulled his hand away and forced himself to make an offer he'd rehearsed for days. *Keep it casual.* "So, it's almost lunchtime. Do you have plans?"

Her mouth dropped for a moment. "No…no plans."

"Would you like to get a quick bite?" Victor shrugged. "Celebrate your first day."

She looked at Gary, as if seeking his approval. "Um…"

Victor grinned. "Gary got lunch his first day too." He turned to him. "And you're invited, by the way." He had only planned to invite Gary if Cara appeared anxious...which she did.

Gary sighed, dramatically. "I wish I could but it's my bi-weekly chiropractor visit. And I *so* need it after the weekend I had."

"Ah, that's right." Victor gave Cara a wry grin. "He hurt his neck a couple months back. Wouldn't tell me what happened. He just showed up Monday morning in a neck brace, muttering something about taking the bus from Atlantic City —"

Gary held up one finger. "Enough!" Then he put his finger down and straightened his posture. "I mean, quiet, if you please, Mr. Barboza."

Victor laughed. He had never asked Gary to be so formal with him, and it amused Victor greatly to mess with him on occasion. Today, Victor was even more thankful for Gary's presence in the office. It was just the tension-breaker he would need in order to calm down enough to subtly woo the new employee.

* * *

Cara tried to do more than stand there, blinking rapidly as if she didn't have a thought in her head. But her mind had indeed gone blank.

Alone, with Victor? Already? She had prepared herself for the idea of working beside him in the same office. But going to lunch was entirely different. They would enjoy a meal together. Alone. Like a date. And she hadn't been on a date in a very, very long time.

"So?" Victor asked patiently. "Lunch?"

Cara inhaled a slightly trembling breath, willing herself to say the thing he wanted to hear. "Lunch. Yes. That'd be fine."

"Great." Victor grinned, then abruptly turned in the direction of his office. "Meet me at the elevator in fifteen minutes." And then he disappeared inside and shut the door.

She put her head down and walked straight to her desk. Her short interaction with Victor had temporarily made her forget about what Rhonda had told her in the break room. But now that she remembered, her time was limited. When she reached her desk, she took out her phone to do a search for "Victor Barboza engagement." In the days since Victor offered her this job, she had searched for him online and found nothing but the company's official website, or other boring links that told her almost nothing. And she knew better than to use his company's Internet connection for a search like this.

It took a few minutes, but she finally found the name "Alexis Whitt" listed along with "Victor Barboza." There appeared to be a wedding website that was no longer functioning, but there was still a wedding gift registry at Michael C. Fina that had not been canceled. Cara's mouth had just dropped open at the sight of a set of sterling silver napkin rings that cost a thousand dollars when she was startled by a knock at the door.

"Hello?" Victor entered her office. "Need to cancel already?"

"No, not at all." She glanced at the clock. She should have been at the elevator by now. "I'm sorry. I lost track of time."

"You sure? When I saw you with your phone I thought maybe your son was sick. How's he doing, by the way?"

Cara picked up her purse and slid her phone inside, then stood from her chair to follow Victor out. "He's doing very well. Thanks for asking. You'd never know he was sick now."

Victor chuckled. "They recover quickly at that age, yes?"

"Yes." She followed him to the elevator, her purse slung over her shoulder. "A little too quickly, in fact. He's still supposed to rest but we can't get him to sit still."

CHAPTER SIX

Cara and Victor chatted as they walked, making them both feel more at ease. There was no other subject that got Cara talking more than Isaac, and Victor was quite happy to continue asking questions. Not only was he amused by the precocious young boy, but he loved to hear Cara speak. This was the closest they had had to a real conversation since they first met, and it was just now that Victor began to realize how much he enjoyed Cara's voice caressing his ears.

Soon they were sitting at the last small table at his favorite deli. With the bustle of people all around them, Victor took the opportunity to scoot his chair closer so they could talk without raising their voices over the noise. Or at least, that's what he'd have her believe.

There was a question that he couldn't bring himself to ask. Each time it seemed there was an opportunity to slip it into the conversation, he stopped.

What's the situation with Isaac's father?

Hell, it was probably considered a personal question that

could get Victor in trouble for violating an employment law. But he was dying to know.

After about a minute of eating in silence, Cara gently dropped her fork to her plate. "With all due respect, Mr. Barboza, I need to ask. Am I a charity case to you?"

Victor wiped his mouth and finished chewing. "Well, that's quite a subject change."

"Please, I need to know. I already took the job and I plan to stay. But you could at least tell me the truth now. Did you hire me out of pity?"

Victor shook his head and put his elbows on the table. "Let's get a few things straight." He cleared his throat. "First, you don't need to be so formal with me. I'm only a few years older than you. Please, call me Victor."

"But Gary doesn't—"

"I know, and I tried to get him to call me by my first name too but he said it didn't feel professional, being that he's my assistant. So, I got used to it. I'd prefer not to get used to it with you." He smiled. "And second, you're not a charity case. You're obviously a strong woman and I most certainly did not hire you out of pity. When I was twelve, my mother moved me and my brothers from Guadalajara to a small town in Texas, outside San Antonio. It was a little ranch town, and we'd been asked to live there if we'd work on his ranch." He let out a friendly chuckle. "It may have been a legal gray area for the ranch owner to have three kids and their mother living there, working for room and board. But it was a hell of a lot better than what we were used to. That man became like a father to me and my brothers. He paid our way through college. I wouldn't be where I am today without his act of kindness."

"Why did he do that?"

"Believe it or not, it was because of my little brother, Armando. The man, Henry Platt, said my brother was nice to him when he'd gotten lost one day, doing some kind of business deal in the town where we lived. He never forgot about it, even after he went home. So, he came back several years later, tracked him down and offered him a job. Pretty soon, we all moved there."

"I've never heard of anything like that before. So that's what you're doing with me? Paying the good deed forward?"

Victor's eyes locked on Cara's. How was he to answer this question? And why did she always have to be so direct? He chose to let his actions speak for a second, holding her gaze a bit longer than necessary until he thought he saw her expression change from suspicious to curious. Then, for the briefest of moments, he let his eyes fall down to the expanse of skin at her neck, her collarbone, then a little further down to the top of her ample cleavage. When his eyes snapped back up to meet hers again, he gave her a half-cocked smile and said, "I told you before—you ask too many questions."

Cara's cheeks immediately flushed a light shade of pink. She looked away at nothing and reached for her drink.

Amused, Victor leaned forward in his chair and watched with intent as her sumptuous lips curved perfectly around her straw.

Perhaps this is enough for today, he thought. He merely wanted to pique her interest and give her a scant clue about his true intentions. And he knew he was treading a fine line. A stubborn woman like Cara would certainly be the type to file a sexual harassment complaint against him. It wasn't as if that sort of accusation could ruin his career, but it could ruin his reputation with Cara. The last thing he wanted was to scare her off by being too bold, or make her think he wanted some kind of sexual repayment for the good deed he'd performed. He just wanted to get to know her, and be near her. It wasn't his fault she was in a bad situation when he found her. It was only too easy for him to fix it, and no matter what happened between them in the future, he would never regret giving her a job.

For now, he simply had to observe her responses and plan his next move.

* * *

Alexis Whitt couldn't believe her eyes.

When she saw Victor cross the street with the full-figured blonde, she had assumed it was a business meeting. Victor was a creature of habit, frequenting the same three restaurants at lunchtime. His penchant for routine was something she both loved and loathed about him.

But when she entered the deli and saw Victor cozying up to the stranger at the small round table, looking at her like there was no one else in the room, Alexis almost shrieked.

She missed that look. And she'd do anything for him to gaze at *her* that way again.

She ran back out of the deli and hid across the street where she could watch them leave and keep an eye on the lobby entrance at Victor's company.

Lunchtime came and went, and Alexis was still standing there behind a stone column, waiting for Victor to exit the deli. But when she saw Gary, she had an even better idea. She waited several minutes, hopefully giving him enough time to take the elevator to his floor and get situated at his desk.

And then she called.

"*Good afternoon, Monarch Enterprises. How may I assist you?*" Gary's voice was chipper as usual.

"Hello, Gary. I'd like to speak with Victor Barboza, please."

"*Oh.*" He let out a disgusted sigh. Under his breath, but loud enough for her to hear, he said, "*I obviously should've looked at the number first.*" His voice got louder. "*To what is this pertaining, Ms. Whitt? Do you have an appointment?*"

"I don't need a meeting. I just need to speak with him. We have some important business to discuss."

"Oh, I'm sure. Give me the details and I'll be sure to give him the message."

"Can you put me through to his voicemail?"

"No, I cannot."

She wanted to scream at him but she wouldn't give him the satisfaction of getting her riled up. In a deliberately calm voice, she said, "Well, I have some information he'll need. It's about a woman I saw him with at lunch. I've known her for years and she's trouble. He needs to know."

Gary chuckled sarcastically. *"Really? You're already trying to get her fired again?"*

"What do you mean, again?"

He sighed loudly. *"Have a lovely afternoon, Ms. Whitt."* And then he hung up.

Fired…again? Confused, Alexis put her phone in her purse and looked at the deli. Seconds later, she saw them exit, both of them smiling, but Victor doing most of the talking.

She shrank back, watching, studying the portly blonde who only seemed vaguely familiar. As if Alexis was meant to hear it, a hint of the strange woman's voice floated her way, just loud enough to bring back a recent memory.

No, it couldn't be her—the girl from the catering company?

She took her phone from her purse and held it up to take a few pictures. She said to herself, quietly, "Oh Victor, have you really stooped to this level? Or maybe you're just hard up." She groaned. "No, it must be more than that."

She was instantly flooded with theories. Maybe he'd known her all along. Maybe that's why there was such a familiarity that night when they were joking at the table.

Alexis felt her blood pressure rising. Had she been played that night? Was this his pathetic way of trying to pay her back for cheating on him while they were engaged?

It didn't matter. Alexis had enough information to pass along to a private investigator who could get this straightened out. No, Victor couldn't possibly be interested in this cow who looked like she'd given up on herself long ago. She would get this woman out of his life just as easily as swatting a fly.

* * *

Cara's new outfit now felt too heavy for such a warm day, especially outside in the hot sun with a sexy man by her side.

She tried to resist it, but how could she not be attracted to Victor? He was tall, dark and gorgeous, and unless she was hallucinating, she swore he was giving her signals that he was interested in her, too.

Maybe Marcy was right, she thought. *Maybe he really was checking me out in the interview last week.*

And she knew darn well he was checking her out today.

At least she was starting to feel more comfortable around him. The conversation flowed easily, and Cara was surprised by how humble and tender he portrayed himself.

But she'd been fooled in the past. She wasn't so naive. There absolutely had to be another reason for his kindness.

Cara and Victor chatted as they entered the building and took the private elevator to their floor. Thankfully, the elevator moved fast and she didn't have more than a minute to fantasize about him pinning her to the corner. She took a few slow, calming breaths and went on with their friendly banter. When they exited the elevator he gave her one last smile before opening his office door.

Clutching her purse to have something else to focus on, she rushed to her own office. Her immediate plan was to resume her Internet stalking.

She had just shoved her purse in a drawer when Gary appeared in front of her desk.

"Hey." He looked over his shoulder then shut the door behind him. "We need to talk."

"Okay."

Gary took a seat in a chair against the wall, his elbows on his knees. He leaned forward as he pushed a button on his headset and shoved the mouthpiece away. "Watch your back around here."

Cara's stomach knotted. "Is this about my talk with Rhonda?"

"Oh God." He winced a little. "Rhonda in acquisitions?"

"Yeah. But she said you're friends. Did I say too much?"

Gary winced in pain for only a split second. "What'd you tell her?"

"That I worked here for Mr. Barboza. Nothing else, really. She told me I needed to lie to people and say I'm a consultant or everyone in the office will start talking because he has a new employee."

"That's all?"

"Yes, I swear."

"Hmm." Gary clucked his tongue against the roof of his mouth. "It's gotta be something else then. And by the way, Rhonda and I *are* friends, in a way, but I never tell her anything about work."

Cara laughed. "Yeah, I could tell she's a gossip. Believe me, I don't wanna do anything to risk losing this job. I'll keep my distance."

Gary shrugged. "Just don't tell her about anything going on here, at work, with Mr. Barboza. She's cool about everything else."

"What'd you mean a second ago when you said it's gotta be

something else? Why'd you come in here and tell me to watch my back?"

He breathed deeply and glanced at the door as if someone were listening. "You and I need to have this talk. I was gonna wait till tomorrow since he'll be out of the office. But oh well." He squared his shoulders, eyes perking up. "Since we'll be working together, we need to get a few things straight. My first priority is taking care of Mr. Barboza. I have the best job in the city and I know it. I get paid well. I have a cool boss who's not around most of the time." He smiled. "And also, I want a job like his someday. He's given me much more responsibility lately along with extra training. He's amazing." He sighed. "So anyway, I will not jeopardize any of it by running my mouth with the hens over there in acquisitions."

She giggled at his hen comment. "I understand. You think he'd fire you for that?"

"Not necessarily, but I know he hates that sort of thing. If he had reason to believe I was leaking any kind of information from his clients he'd probably have me transferred down to the mail room. That's like dying and going to hell around here." He groaned. "But anyway, back to the reason I came in here. I received a disturbing phone call a few minutes ago. It was from his ex-fiancee." His mouth formed a distinct frown. "She's bad news."

"What's her name?"

"Alexis Whitt. Of the Whitt Foundation."

"Whitt Foundation? The same people who hosted the dinner where I got fired?" Cara's jaw dropped. She already knew Alexis's name but hadn't made the connection until now. "Was she the woman he was sitting with?"

Gary raised a brow. "They were sitting together?"

"Yeah. Beautiful woman with red hair. Really snooty."

Gary nodded. "That's her."

"That witch got me fired."

"Doesn't surprise me. Apparently, she saw you two at lunch together. She called while you were gone, acting like she had inside information on the person he was with. *You.*"

Cara brought her hand to her chest. "Is she trying to get me fired? Again? What the heck did I ever do to her?"

Gary shook his head. "Don't worry. She's jealous. Grasping at straws."

"She's rich and she has everything! Why would someone like that try to ruin my life?"

"Oh, honey." Gary smirked. "Rich people don't have everything. Trust me. I deal with hundreds of them, daily. Seems like the more money you have, the crazier you are."

"Is Victor crazy?"

"Maybe. But not in a bad way." He laughed.

Cara let out a sad sigh. "So, he really did hire me as a charity case. He felt bad because his fiancee got me fired."

"Ex-fiancee." Just then, the phone rang and Gary stood up. He walked over to Cara and gave her shoulder a friendly pat. "And I think your hiring involved a little more than that." Gary moved the mouthpiece down to his lips and hurried to the door. "Good afternoon, Monarch Enterprises…" He left her office and walked to his desk as he spoke to a client.

I'm even more confused than I was before, Cara thought.

To clear her mind, she took a moment to check her personal email on her phone.

"Huh?" She blinked, disbelieving the message she had just received. It was from her former manager in Chicago. The subject read, "Need a job?" The body of the email simply said, "Call me when you get this."

Cara closed her office door before dialing.

"*Cara? Is that you?*"

"Justine? How are you? I just got your email and—"

Justine's voice was hushed. *"I'm great. Don't have much time though. I just stepped out of a meeting to take your call."* Her voice became slightly louder. *"Any chance you want your old job back?"*

"You've got to be kidding me. I just started a brand new job today."

"Oh, shoot! I thought you were a sure thing."

"What happened? I thought the company was on its way out."

"Apparently not. We were acquired by Emilieu Global."

"No!" Cara walked to her chair and sat down.

"Yes. There were rumors for a long time but it just became official today. They work very fast. They already had new operating budgets waiting when they met with senior level management today. They added fifty new positions to the headcount with more on the way. I was so hoping to bring you back."

Cara whined to herself and pressed her palm against her forehead. "I can't believe this. Of course it would happen the day I start a new job."

"I'm sure you can still quit the new job."

The logical side of Cara told her to take the job in Chicago. She and Isaac were stable there. And she loved working with Justine. But when she thought about Victor, her answer was clear. "I'm sorry. I can't do it. If this had happened a week ago or even a few days ago, I'd probably already be packing boxes. I have to stay here. I need to see what develops."

With a dramatic sigh, Justine said, *"Fine. But if you change your mind in the next…I don't know…couple weeks? Month? You let me know."*

"I will."

71

CHAPTER SEVEN

Cara opened the front door on Friday evening and entered the house with a sigh of relief. Her feet hurt and she was dying to slip out of her body shaper and into some comfy sweatpants. "I'm home!"

Isaac ran to her from the kitchen. "Mommy Mommy Mommy!"

She picked him up and gave him a kiss. "Were you a good boy for Grandma today?"

He gave her a mischievous grin and said, "Yes," then threw his face against her neck.

Cara had a feeling he was lying, but she was quickly distracted by rich aromas wafting from the kitchen. She gently lowered Isaac to the floor and he ran off to the living room. "Mom, what are you making?"

Patty's eyes brightened when she saw her daughter appear. She reached for a potholder and opened the oven. "Nothing much. Lasagna. Garlic bread."

A glance around the room piqued Cara's curiosity. On the

kitchen counter, she saw some of her mother's recipes that were only used for holidays and special occasions. Homemade garlic bread, Grandma Sylvia's special red sauce, among others.

When Patty saw Cara touch the recipes, she snatched them from her hand. "I need those."

"What's going on? Is it someone's birthday I don't know about?"

"No." Patty smiled. "We're…um…just celebrating your first week at your new job."

"Oh." Cara returned her smile. "That's sweet. I hadn't thought of that. Is Marcy coming over?"

"No."

"Well, I'll invite her. I don't think she's working tonight."

"No!"

"Why not?"

"Just…no. Not tonight. Trust me."

Cara shook her head and turned to leave the kitchen. "Fine, whatever. I'm too tired to argue. I'm gonna go get comfortable."

"Don't get too comfortable. Wear something decent."

Cara spun around to face her. She knew that tone in her meddling mother's voice. "Okay. You're up to something. What is it?"

Patty shrugged and focused her attention on a mixing bowl on the counter. "Nothing."

"You're lying. What's going on? Did you invite someone over?" Cara raised her eyebrows. "Is it Stanley, that guy you met in the park a few weeks ago who you don't think I know about?"

Patty's lips pursed as a pink hue flooded her cheeks. She whisked the ingredients in the bowl. "That was nothing."

"Oh, come on, mom. You're a hot grandma." Cara was glad

she talked Patty into dyeing her hair recently. The new dark brown color covered Patty's gray and made her look ten years younger, by Cara's estimation.

"Go keep your son occupied while I finish up in here, okay? I've had to fight him away from the fridge all afternoon since he saw me put the cake in there."

Cara groaned. "What the heck, Mom? I'm not leaving until you tell me what's going on."

Patty let the whisk drop to the bowl. "Fine." She looked in her daughter's eyes. "Your boss is joining us for dinner."

"What?" Cara gasped. "No! You can't!"

Patty gave her a lighthearted grin. "Too late now. He'll be here in…" She glanced at the clock on the wall. "About an hour. Said he had a late business meeting then he'd be on his way over."

Cara was too stunned to speak for a moment. She had barely seen Victor since their lunch on Monday because he had been visiting clients or having closed-door meetings in his office. She had determined by now that Victor merely hired her to get back at Alexis Whitt. "Mom, this is a bad idea for *so* many reasons. You shouldn't have called him."

"I didn't. He called here. Said he wanted to make sure Isaac was okay. Then we started talking." Her eyes lit up. "He practically invited himself over."

"Why would he do that? He could ask me about Isaac anytime."

"Because he likes you! That's why."

"He doesn't like me, Mom. He's trying to make a point to his ex. That's why he hired me."

Patty shrugged. "Whatever. Doesn't matter the reason. If he wants to give you some attention, you should let him."

Cara threw her hands in the air. "Who knows? Maybe you're right. I hadn't thought about it that way."

"Yes. See? You should listen to your mother more often."

Cara grumbled to herself and left the kitchen.

An hour later, the doorbell rang, rustling the butterflies in Cara's stomach. She had changed into a pair of black pants and a loose-fitting light blue blouse. Her long hair hung in soft curls down her back.

As Patty went for the door, Cara gave Isaac another inspection to make sure he wasn't sticky or dirty.

"Mommy," he said, "cake?"

Cara winced. She could tell from his whiny tone that they might be in for one of his rare tantrums. She knelt down to look in his eyes. "If you be good you can have cake after dinner, okay?"

He pouted. "Cake now."

She kissed his forehead. "Not now. After dinner with everyone else." She stood and took Isaac's hand, leading him to the front door when she heard Victor speaking with Patty. *Please be good, Isaac*, she silently pleaded.

Victor's mesmerizing eyes met hers immediately when she and Isaac entered the dining room. He held her gaze for a long moment then said, "Hi, Cara. Hope it's okay that I came by for dinner."

The nerves in her stomach tightened, but she tried to appear calm. She noticed he was wearing a long-sleeved white dress shirt with cufflinks, like he'd left his jacket and tie in the car. The shirt was fitted perfectly, as if it were molded just for his athletic, muscular body. "Yes, it's fine."

Victor held up a gift bag. "I brought something for Isaac." He looked down in Isaac's direction, smiling. "Hello?"

Cara felt a sharp tug on the back of her pants. Isaac had grabbed a handful of the fabric as he hid behind her leg. She patted the top of his head and looked at Victor. "Sorry, he's shy around new people lately."

"It's just a phase." Patty touched Victor's arm. "I need to go to the kitchen. Make yourself at home."

Victor nodded and turned his attention to Isaac. "Hi there. We spoke on the phone."

Isaac hugged Cara's leg with all his might and looked down at the floor.

Cara's voice was gentle. "Do you remember talking on the phone?"

Isaac shook his head.

"Come on," she said. "Sure you do. It's Victor."

Isaac paused, then loudly whispered, "Bictow."

Victor chuckled and picked up a gift bag he had set down behind him. "I have a present for you, Isaac."

Cara's eyebrows furrowed at Victor. "You didn't have to do that."

"I wanted to." Victor reached inside the bag and produced a large plastic yellow car with a red stripe all the way around. He knelt down to Isaac's level. "This is for you. You told me you like cars."

Isaac squealed. He let go of Cara's leg and grabbed the car from Victor with both arms. "Wace caw!" He stomped his feet, giggling.

Cara melted inside at the sight of her boss, down on his knees in his designer pants, smiling at her son. "Isaac, what do you say when someone gives you a present?"

Isaac held out the car, examining it. Then he looked at Victor. "You wike wace caws?"

"Yes," Victor said. "I love race cars."

Isaac smiled and softly said, "You have a wace caw?"

"No," Cara said. "You know what to say when someone gives you a present. Say, 'thank you.'"

Isaac hugged the car and whispered, "Thank you."

"You're welcome," Victor said.

"You have a wace caw?" Isaac asked again.

Cara shook her head. "I'm sorry. He's obsessed with race cars lately."

"It's okay," Victor said, beaming at Isaac. "I have a car outside. You wanna see it?"

"Yeah!" Isaac ran past Victor to fetch his shoes from the rack inside the front door, letting his new toy fall to the floor with a loud *thunk*.

Victor stood, wincing at Cara. "I'm sorry. I probably shouldn't have done that."

"It's fine." Cara was already worried about how she would get her son back inside for dinner.

Isaac ran outside with Victor in tow as soon as the door opened. This was the first time Cara set eyes on Victor's car. It was sleek and sporty and had a symbol on the front she had never seen before.

Patty soon joined Cara as they hovered nearby, watching Victor open the door to let Isaac sit inside.

"They get along so well," Patty said. "You can tell he'd be a great father."

Cara gritted her teeth. "You're thinking too far ahead. I don't want Isaac getting attached to him."

Patty held back the words she really wanted to say. "Well, it's good for him to have a man around once in a while." She knew her daughter was too protective of herself. They had argued about it dozens of times, and tonight she just wanted Cara to loosen up and try to let her guard down.

They both smiled as they watched Isaac's eyes dance around the inside of the fancy car. Victor stood over him, pointing out things that made Isaac *ooh* and *ah*. After a minute, Victor stepped away, laughing and holding the door open while Isaac gripped the steering wheel and made his own sound effects as if he were driving.

Patty waited a while longer then went back inside to finish setting up for dinner.

Cara walked up to the car. "Having a good time?"

Isaac nodded gleefully, puffing out his lips as he made a "*Vroom vroom*" sound.

Cara whispered to Victor, "The only time he can almost pronounce his R is when he's saying '*vroom vroom*.'"

Victor laughed.

"Okay, sweetie." Cara looked at Isaac. "We have to go inside for dinner now."

Isaac stuck out his bottom lip and strengthened his grip on the steering wheel.

"Oh no," Cara mumbled. She thought for sure Isaac was about to screech at the top of his lungs. "Remember the chocolate cake? You can have it if you go inside for dinner."

Isaac ignored her, but he stared thoughtfully at the dashboard like he was considering his options.

Victor extended his hand to Isaac. "Come on. Let's go eat. I want some of that cake."

Isaac gave Victor a quizzical glance, then waited a moment and suddenly reached for his hand and hopped out of the car. "Awwight." He let out a dramatic huff as he started toward the house, pulling Victor along.

"Wait, let me lock up." Victor chuckled and closed the door, then walked along with Isaac and Cara. "They're a lot of fun at this age, huh?"

Cara narrowed her eyes. "Depends on which day you ask me. I never know what to expect."

"Seems like he's fully recovered from surgery."

"Yeah, seems that way. He's still healing but you'd never know it."

Isaac stopped, looking up at Victor. "See?" He opened his mouth and stuck out his tongue. "No tonsahs."

Victor nodded. "Yes, I see."

Cara sighed. "He always knows when we're talking about him."

They went inside the house where Patty had dinner waiting. Patty also made sure that she and Isaac sat together across the table while Cara and Victor sat side by side.

Isaac did the most talking during dinner, regaling Victor with tales that were sometimes hard to understand. Some were true stories. Some were based on true stories. Others were entirely fabricated. Through it all, Victor was thoroughly entertained.

Cara was glad, for once, that her son was in a talkative mood. It removed some of the pressure from this awkward situation.

After dinner, the four of them moved to the living room where they talked and had dessert. Isaac was thrilled to finally eat the chocolate cake he'd been waiting for. Cara was afraid he would want to go outside and see Victor's car again, but around eight o'clock he started to yawn and said he was tired.

Patty winked at Cara. "We went to the park today and he didn't take a nap. He's worn out." Patty forced a yawn. "And so am I, come to think about it." She turned to Isaac. "I think me and you better go upstairs, don't you?"

Isaac gave her a lazy nod.

"Good night, Isaac," Victor said.

Isaac grinned. "Good night, Bictow. Good night Mommy."

Cara smirked at Patty, who wouldn't look at Cara as she followed Isaac out of the room. Cara knew Patty wasn't tired. She was just trying to leave her alone with Victor.

As soon as they left, Victor inched slightly closer to Cara on the sofa. "Looks like I made a new friend tonight."

"Yeah. He doesn't usually take to adults so quickly. Are you around children a lot?"

"No. Almost never, in fact." Victor shrugged. "I guess we just click."

"Hmm. So, tell me." She positioned herself so she was facing him. "Did you go to Gary's house the week you hired him, too?"

With a weak smile he said, "Uh…no. No, I didn't."

"So, this isn't normal new employee procedure? Like taking me out to lunch my first day?"

He undid the first button of his shirt and flexed his neck, trying to get more comfortable. He smiled at her question. "No, not exactly."

"Then what are you doing here? Calling my mom, giving my son a present. Hanging out after dinner in this house." She cocked her head to the side. "What's your game? Why are you doing this?"

"Maybe I'm just a nice guy."

"No, I don't think that's it."

He smirked. "Thanks."

"That's not what I meant. What I mean is, I don't know why you're being so nice to me. It's not normal."

"Cara." He looked deep in her eyes. "You're an intelligent woman. Do I really need to spell it out for you?"

"Spell out what? That you're using me to get back at Alexis Whitt?"

Victor jolted out of his relaxed position and sat up straight. "Whoa. Where the hell'd you get that?"

"Does it matter? It's true, isn't it?"

He scoffed. "No. Not at all. She and I've been over for a while now. We were probably over way before I…Didn't your mom say there was wine chilling in the fridge?"

Cara was about to respond when Victor stood and turned in the direction of the kitchen. "Hey!" She followed him.

He was already turning on the light in the kitchen when she caught up.

"What are you doing?" she asked.

"Getting some wine. Patty said to make myself at home. So, I'm making myself at home. I'll get the wine if you get the glasses. I don't know where they are."

Cara rolled her eyes and opened the cabinet to get one goblet. She set it on the counter with a light *clink*.

Victor took the bottle from the refrigerator. "I need a corkscrew." He squinted at the lone glass on the counter. "Where's yours?"

"I don't want any."

"Yeah, you do." He reached up to the cabinet where he saw Cara get the first goblet. "Corkscrew, please."

She groaned and found it in a drawer. "I'm off the clock, you know. I don't really have to do what you say right now."

"And yet, you are." He picked up the corkscrew, smiling.

"That's only because you're my guest and I don't wanna be rude."

"You, rude?" He narrowed one eye, his tone clearly sarcastic. "Never."

She rolled her eyes and looked away as he opened the bottle and poured them each a glass. He handed one to her.

"For you, *senorita*," he said. "Drink up."

Cara felt weak in the knees when she heard the way *senorita* rolled so effortlessly from his tongue. No man had ever addressed her like that. She took the goblet and raised it to her lips, ready to drink.

"Oh wait." He extended his glass to hers. "We didn't toast."

She stopped. "What's the occasion? To what do we toast?"

Victor rubbed his jaw, thinking. "Race cars."

After a brief hesitation, she laughed.

"What's wrong?" he asked. "Did I overstep my bounds with Isaac?"

She lowered the glass and took a deep breath. "I don't know…"

"Are you afraid to let him get attached to me?"

Her brows knitted as she tried to think of something to say. "Uh…"

"Is that what happened with his dad? Did he leave you and Isaac?"

She gulped. "Not exactly. Why are you asking me this? I don't understand you at all. That's a very personal question and you barely even know me."

Victor watched her eyes as he took a slow sip of his wine. He knew he'd hit a sensitive part of her past. "I have almost no memories of my own father. That's why I ask. I'm not trying to make you uncomfortable. Why do you always look so anxious around me?"

Cara cocked her head to the side. "Gee, I don't know. Maybe because my life's been a roller coaster since I met you? I get fired from one job and laid off from another. Suddenly I'm working for you and I'm not even sure what I'm supposed to be doing all day. Oh, and you pop up at my house, give my son gifts, talk to my mom without me knowing about it." Her eyes were wide. "Why would a guy like you come all the way to Newark to have dinner on a Friday night?"

"What? All the way to Newark? It's not that far." His voice softened. "Has it occurred to you that maybe I simply *like* you?"

She fidgeted, tucking her hair behind her ear as her eyes wandered around the room. "No. That's not possible. I saw the kind of woman you date."

Gently, he covered her hand with his. "I don't know what

you heard, but she and I are over. Completely over. And that's all I'm going to say about it."

She wiggled her hand away. "Well, something doesn't make sense. Men like you are never interested in women like me without having an agenda."

"What's that supposed to mean? Why wouldn't I be interested in a woman like you? You shouldn't be so down on yourself."

"I'm not down on myself. I'm realistic."

He leaned down to her until his face was inches from hers. "You know what? The only thing I find unattractive about you is your attitude about yourself." He nudged Cara's wine toward her. "Drink. Loosen up a little."

She glared up at him. "Why should I?"

"Because I'd like to get you drunk and have my way with you." He laughed, knowing she had no idea whether he was serious.

She wanted to be stubborn. For a second she imagined throwing her wine in his face and telling him to get lost. But a stronger desire quickly took over. One that made her forget her desperate urge to resist him. With her eyes firmly set on his, she brought the glass to her lips and tipped the bottom of it to the ceiling.

"More?" he asked.

Her voice was weak. "Yes."

Victor poured more wine for her.

Cara drank the contents in one swallow.

He smiled. "Another?"

"No." She plunked the goblet down.

"Good." Victor put his hand under her chin and tilted her face up to his. "If you make me wait any longer I think I may have to fire you." And then he bent down and covered her mouth with his. His tongue quickly parted her lips and slipped in between.

She melted into his arms, unable to control her reaction.

His hands went to her hair, his fingers trailing through her soft tendrils until he felt the weight of her breasts against him. He instantly pulled her closer and kissed her harder. His hands slid down her back to lift up her blouse.

She shuddered when she felt the tips of his fingers digging against her body shaper like he wanted to tear it off. But she was too mesmerized by his kiss to be embarrassed. If he was put off by the extra weight she carried, he didn't show it. His urgent tongue fiercely licked the inside of her lips as his hands worked even lower, slipping under her waistband to the fleshy rise of her backside.

Damn it, Cara thought. *If I'd known he wanted me like this I wouldn't have worn my shaper.*

She forgot to resist him; she forgot about analyzing his motives. Her body was alive, her senses ignited by his longing for her. It didn't matter where it came from or how long it would last. She knew she'd be a fool not to let him ravish her.

As her arms tightly clutched his body she felt one of his hands drift up her back and around her waist, then cupping her breast.

He pulled away from her for a moment, only long enough for them each to take a breath. Cara couldn't stop her throat from letting out a deep moan. Victor's mouth instinctively went back to hers as his hands resumed their exploration.

That's when they heard the sound of tiny footsteps enter the kitchen.

They pulled away from each other with a gasp.

"Mommy." Isaac frowned as held his stomach. "Tummy."

Cara's eyes flashed between Isaac and Victor, wondering what her son had seen. She ran to Isaac. "You're sick?"

Patty entered the kitchen. "Isaac! Why didn't you come to my room?" She looked at Cara. "I'm so sorry. I should've run out of my bedroom the second I thought I heard his door open. I'll take care of him." She glanced at Cara with wide eyes, then took Isaac's hand and led him out of the kitchen.

Victor winced and mumbled, "I'm sorry."

"It's okay," Cara said.

"No, it's not." He looked outside the room to make sure Patty and Isaac were gone, then walked to Cara. He stroked her cheek with the back of his fingers. "I'm so sorry. I got carried away. I know this is weird for you. I'm your boss and now I'm some creep who's trying to seduce you in your mom's kitchen—"

"Please, it's fine—"

"No." He pressed his palm against the back of her head and whispered in her ear, "I can't believe I did that. You're just so damn beautiful, I couldn't hold back anymore."

"Oh." She closed her eyes, basking in the feel of his warm breath and his compliment.

"I don't know what to do now." He gave her a slow, wet kiss on the cheek before his lips returned to her ear. "I should go. I'm sorry."

Victor was already three steps toward the door before she realized he had walked away.

Cara's eyes popped open and she followed him in silence, her mind racing, too flustered to think of anything to say.

When he reached the door he simply opened it and gave her another kiss on the cheek, then whispered, "See you Monday," in her ear.

"See you Monday." She watched him walk to his car. They exchanged a smile and a wave before he backed out of the driveway.

Cara closed the door and made a beeline for the wine bottle

in the kitchen.

CHAPTER EIGHT

On Monday morning, Cara stayed in her car in the parking garage, in a deep phone call with Marcy. "Now remember, if you go by the house don't say a thing to Mom."

Marcy sighed. *"I won't. How many times do I have to tell you?"*

"Good. She's so nosy. I swear, I gotta move outta that house."

"Give her a break. She only wants to see her daughter in a happy relationship for once."

"It was just a little making out. There's no relationship."

"Maybe not yet…" Marcy chuckled.

"I'm not in the mood for this argument. I have a very awkward day ahead of me and I need to stop procrastinating and go inside."

"It'll be fine. Just follow his lead. If he acts like nothing happened on Friday night, you go along and act like nothing happened. And if he comes to your office and throws you down on the desk because he wants more, you just—"

"I'm too irritated to let you finish that sentence." Cara opened her car door and stepped outside, holding the phone to her ear. "I gotta run. I'm already late…" She stopped talking when she noticed a blue car with dark tinted windows, parked near the elevator. "You ever have the feeling you're being watched?"

"*Watched? By who?*"

Cara squinted, unsuccessfully trying to see through the windshield. She shook her head and quickly looked away, concentrating her effort on getting to the elevator as fast as possible. "Oh, nothing. I think I'm just nervous and paranoid."

"*Calm down. Call me if there're any new developments. Your life's way more interesting than mine right now.*"

"Sure. But I wish mine was a little *less* interesting. Bye." Cara chuckled as she hung up the phone.

A few minutes later, she was relieved to find Victor's office door closed and Gary nowhere in sight. The clock in her office said 8:07. Hopefully nobody would ever know she was a little late. She turned on her computer and was just about to head to the break room for her first cup of coffee when her office phone beeped and Victor's voice sounded.

"*Cara? You there?*"

She gasped, then pressed the intercom button. "Yes?"

His voice was urgent. "*My office. Now.*"

Does he want to pick up where we stopped on Friday night? "I'll be right there."

Cara stood and straightened her skirt, then rushed to Victor's office. Her heart sank when she saw Gary perched attentively on a chair in front of Victor's desk.

Victor spoke aloud to who Cara quickly realized was a client on speakerphone. His expression was all business when his eyes made contact with Cara's. He gestured for her to take a seat beside Gary and went on with his conversation, his hands folded atop his desk. "The exchange rate won't be a factor…" He smirked at Gary as he continued.

Gary smiled and wrote frantically on a notepad.

Cara fidgeted in her seat. She didn't think to bring a notebook. *Was I supposed to know about this meeting? Why does he want me here?*

It went on for a while longer as Cara did her best to follow along. She quickly deduced this was a call with a venture capitalist who was now hesitant about an overseas investment. Victor, however, was charming and kept his cool during the meeting, even making the anxious client laugh a few times.

Gary nodded and interjected answers when Victor deferred to him. But Victor never asked Cara for input, confusing her more than ever. Victor showed no emotion the few times he glanced her way.

Maybe he just wants to watch me drool over him. Cara struggled to keep her eyes from lingering on Victor for long, but it was nearly impossible. He was all she had thought about for days. Watching him work his magic with a client made him even sexier.

When the call ended, Victor shot Gary a wicked grin. "Great way to start a Monday, huh?" he said. "You sure you wanna piece of this business?"

"Absolutely." Gary stood and returned his grin. "I better get started on this report." He read his notebook as he turned around to head to his desk outside the room.

Victor waited until Gary shut the door before his eyes flew to Cara's. His tone was soft. "So, how are you this morning?"

"Um…" Cara stammered, caught off guard by his easy question after the tense phone call. "I'm not quite sure what to say."

"Not quite sure, huh?" He stood up and casually strolled around the desk to sit in the chair where Gary had been. He swiveled it to face her then leaned forward, elbows against his knees. "Tell me the truth. How are you this morning?"

"I don't know. I expected it to be awkward."

"Yeah. Me too. But you know what? I woke up this morning and realized it didn't need to be awkward. I don't *need* to feel embarrassed that I made a pass at you. I don't *need* to be paranoid that you'll try to file sexual harassment charges against me." He chuckled and flashed her a lazy smile. "What I *need* is a way to spend more time with you so we can let things happen naturally. And I think Mr. Kincaid may have just made that possible for me."

Cara was so flustered, it took a few seconds to remember that Mr. Kincaid was the client with whom Victor was speaking. "What?" She swallowed. "More time with me?"

"Yes." Victor held her gaze for another moment then picked up a file on his desk and handed it to Cara. "Familiarize yourself with this company. The Lochmere Group. It's Kincaid and his partners. I'll need you to provide some expertise."

"Me? What about Gary? You're training him to do what you do, right?"

"Yes, but I need him here. He takes care of everyone while I'm out of the office, which is almost constantly these days. From the call just now, you know The Lochmere Group has a lot of political interests and they're afraid of being seen in a negative light for investing in a foreign company. It's not true, though. There will be absolutely no jobs added overseas and the U.S. factories will see significant growth. Anyway, we'll need your public relations help to put the right spin on this endeavor."

Cara cleared her throat, determined to act like she had actually been able to pay attention to the phone call. "Don't they have their own public relations staff?"

"No, actually. It's not a big corporation, just a group of investors. They can either hire a publicist or they can let me take care of it so they'll like me enough to continue to give me their business." He smiled. "So, what do you think? Will Isaac be okay with me taking his mommy away for a few days?"

"What?" Cara's eyes were wide. "You want…me…away… with you? For a few days?"

"Yes. Is that a problem? Because you don't have to go. I won't fire you." He lifted an eyebrow. "I'll be disappointed, but I definitely won't fire you."

Cara gulped. "Are you sure?" Her stomach was suddenly in knots. "Listen, no matter what happens, I really can't afford to lose this job. I—"

"Stop." He put his hand on her knee for a brief moment. "I know what you're gonna say and you have nothing to worry about. If, for some reason, you end up hating me and you don't want to work for me anymore, I'll make sure you still have a job. I promise. I can always have you transferred to another department or find you a job opening with one of my clients. Honestly, don't let yourself be worried about that." He looked in her eyes. "Just say you'll come on this trip to Houston with me. It's only for a night. We'll fly out first thing tomorrow morning. I'll have you back here before the end of the next business day, if all goes well."

"Just so I understand, you want me there because you really need my help?" She paused for a deep breath. "And, you want to spend time with me?"

"Yes. Please, don't be nervous. I don't like to play games." With a lighthearted shrug, he added, "And I guess that means I'm not very good at this. I'm a simple man. I see something I want, I go after it. No games."

"And that's why you offered me this job?"

"That was a coincidence. I knew you had a need. I had a way to fill it. You shouldn't have to struggle unnecessarily. If I'd met you another way, I'd still be interested. Trust me."

She scoffed inwardly. *Trust him? If only it were that easy.*

Victor looked at his watch. "Now, if you'll excuse me, I'll be in meetings the rest of the day." He gently tapped her knee. "Gary will have all the details to you before you go home this evening. That is, if you decide to come. And I hope you will."

Cara watched Victor reach for a folder on his desk, then stand and turn around in the direction of the door. "You're leaving already?"

Victor walked fast. With his hand on the doorknob he glanced at her over his shoulder. "You don't think I'm stupid enough to attack you at work, do you?" He winked. "That's what private planes are for."

* * *

About two hours later, as Cara was browsing online for information about Houston, Rhonda appeared at her door.

"Hey!" Rhonda said. "How's it goin' over here?"

"Pretty good. How are you?"

"Fine. So, you maybe wanna do that lunch today? Welcome you aboard? It's been a week now." Rhonda walked around Cara's desk to stand beside her chair. She gawked at Cara's monitor. "Houston, huh?"

Cara instantly clicked away to a blank browser. "Yeah. Just researching a client."

"Mm hmm." Rhonda's voice got quiet. "I already heard your boss requested the company jet tomorrow. He taking you with him?"

Cara struggled to keep her voice steady and not show her surprise at the question. "I don't know yet."

"Oh." Rhonda's eyebrows shot up. "You don't know yet? You mean, he gave you a choice?"

I should've just said no. Cara mentally kicked herself for what she'd already told Rhonda. Daily, she received subtle warnings from Gary to keep Victor's activities quiet. "No, he's just not sure if he needs me. That's all."

"Oh yeah? Well who's he taking then? His trip request said there were two people. Gary never travels."

A throat cleared. Rhonda and Cara looked up to see Gary in the doorway, head cocked sideways as he glared at Rhonda.

"How'd you hear about the trip request, hmm?" Gary asked. "Sally in accounts payable?"

Rhonda smirked. "If you must know, it was my boss, Mr. Noonan. He was ranting about it in his office because he wanted the jet tomorrow but Barboza beat him to it."

"Well then," Gary said, "I guess Mr. Noonan will have to settle for brushing his legs against the commoners in first class. Or worse." He let out a small gasp and brought his hand to his chest. "Coach!"

Rhonda and Gary shared a hearty laugh as Cara closed the browser Rhonda had caught her using.

After Rhonda settled down, she said, "Well, for what it's worth, if it were me, I'd love to get that man alone in an airplane." She made a grunt of approval. "Yes, Victor Barboza could take me on an airplane. An elevator. A backseat."

Gary's eyes rolled. "I'm aware."

"Oh, please," Rhonda said to Gary. "Don't act like you haven't thought about it."

Gary squared his shoulders, his eyes playful. "Look, you can have your little trashy conversations with the sluts over there in acquisitions but here in Mr. Barboza's department we keep it classy." He grinned.

"Oh, get over yourself. So, how about lunch today?" Rhonda waggled her eyebrows at Cara.

"How rude." Gary scoffed. "I'm standing right here."

Rhonda sighed. "Oh, you can come too, I guess."

"Great," Gary said. "Cara? You in?"

"Sure," Cara said. "You guys pick the restaurant."

"Sounds good to me." Rhonda smiled and walked past Gary to go back to her office. "I have a few things to do before we leave. Meet you guys downstairs at noon."

As soon as she left, Gary stepped outside the door to make sure Rhonda was out of earshot, then he reentered Cara's office and shut the door.

"Okay, she's fishing," Gary said. "That's why I invited myself to lunch, to make sure you don't say anything."

Cara smirked. "I didn't mean to tell her anything, I swear. She looked at my computer—"

"No, no, no. I didn't mean you were untrustworthy. She's just *that* nosy. She'll trick you."

"I don't get it. Why is this such a big deal to everyone around here? It makes me uncomfortable."

"It's because of Alexis Whitt. I've suspected for a while she has some spies around here but I don't know who they are. Could be Rhonda. Either her, or someone in accounting, I think. Someone who sees purchase orders *and* human resources activity." He stared off at the wall, suddenly deep in thought. "Yeah, it'd have to be."

"So, that's why I have to be careful who I talk to and what I say? Because Alexis has spies around here?"

He shrugged. "Well, that, and the fact that Mr. Barboza's always a topic of conversation. I mean, think about it. He's young and single. Of the three partners here at Monarch, he's the only one who doesn't have a whole department reporting to him. He has me, and now you." Gary chuckled. "Believe me, rumors were flying when he hired me, too."

"You mean, people thought…you and him?"

"Yes." He nodded. "Yes, they did. And it didn't help that I made the mistake of telling someone how hot I thought he was."

Cara laughed out loud. "Oh no."

"Yes." Gary let out an exasperated sigh. "I won't make that mistake again. The rumors were already going but I sure didn't help. That's when I found out how much Mr. Barboza likes to stay out of the office gossip. He doesn't care what people say until it affects him somehow, and one of the other partners mentioned it to him. That's when he sat me down and told me he didn't have time for drama and he expected me to keep everything private in this office."

"He actually approached you about it?"

"Yes. But the odd thing is, he thought it was kind of funny that anyone thought he and I were an item." He chuckled for a few moments then cleared his throat. "We had a similar talk before you started. He wanted to make sure the rumors were kept to a minimum. He said it was to keep you from feeling uncomfortable around here." He smiled. "Mr. Barboza cares *very* much about your comfort."

Cara put her elbows on her desk, palms against her forehead. "I don't know what to think, Gary! This is crazy! A few weeks ago I didn't even know him and now I work for him? He cares about my comfort? Whatever that means." She groaned. "And he wants to take me on an overnight trip." She looked up at him. "*Tomorrow.* I've only worked here for a week but he wants me to travel with him, *tomorrow*? What's going on? Is it because of Alexis? He wants revenge on her that badly?"

Gary shook his head. "Honey, I really don't know what to tell you." He winked. "But if I were you, I'd be on the plane tomorrow." He reached for the door. "I have to go take care of a few things before lunch. See you at noon."

Cara's first instinct was to calm her nerves by calling Marcy, but she could already hear Marcy's voice saying, "Loosen up and take the trip."

Maybe she's right. Cara felt her palms sweating as she imagined being alone with Victor in close quarters.

CHAPTER NINE

Silence. Two whole minutes of silence had passed since either Cara or Victor had spoken a word. Neither had anticipated the sexually charged thoughts that would go through each of their minds as they sat across from each other on the small plane.

To distract herself, Cara spread out the Lochmere file on the tiny table between them and pored over the documents for the tenth time. Every time she looked at him, Victor was either staring at her or gazing out the window like he was annoyed with her.

Do I want him to make a move? That was the question she pondered since yesterday morning's meeting…including a very restless night; she had lain wide awake for hours, tossing and turning as fantasies consumed her.

Victor put his elbows on the table and leaned forward. "You sure you don't want a drink? It might help."

"No." Caught off-guard, Cara gasped under her breath. Every time he moved she caught a subtle hint of his cologne. It didn't seem like his usual scent. It smelled more sensual and earthy, like he had worn it just to seduce her.

Cara swallowed hard and repeated herself. "No. I shouldn't drink before seeing a client. I don't hold my liquor well. I would hate to make a bad impression."

"Ah." A corner of Victor's mouth turned up. "Well, the flight will take another two hours, and our meeting is another hour after that. You have plenty of time to rest and get back to normal before then. You can even take a nap, if you want."

Although she had been assured the pilot could not hear them, paranoia caused Cara to quiet her voice. "Oh really? Is that your thing? Get me to pass out and then you'll do whatever you want to me?"

Victor's amused eyes narrowed. "I'd rather have you awake."

"Are you serious?" Cara sat up straight, trying to appear indifferent to his advances. "You really just brought me here to hit on me? I'm good at my job and I'd love a chance to prove that."

"I know you're good at your job. I wouldn't have hired you otherwise." Victor placed his glass on the table and took a seat beside Cara, carefully sliding an arm behind her back. "I tire of games very quickly, *querida*."

Instinctively, Cara turned to face him. She held his gaze for only a moment before the want in his eyes became too much to bear. When she felt his fingers stroking her face, she shut her eyes tight, determined to keep the promise she had made to herself the night before.

Just. Let. Go.

Maybe Victor's intentions didn't matter as much as she originally thought. How many times in her life would something like this ever happen to her? Why should she try to fight it when her body was already shouting *yes*?

Cara's heartbeat quickened when she felt his hot breath

against her forehead. His fingers traced a line under her jaw then down to her collarbone. They had almost reached the top of her breasts when they turned back, running up to the nape of her neck.

Victor tilted Cara's face up to his and kissed her.

Her deep moan was squelched in his kiss. His mouth was bolder than their previous encounter. In the light of day with no one around to distract her, she sensed his desire. His lips were sneaky and possessive, matching her every move. His tongue slowly crept between her lips as he unbuttoned her jacket and slid it off one shoulder, exposing the camisole she wore underneath.

Cara's hand was on Victor's back, her fingers digging against his shirt to feel his sleek muscles. There was nothing stopping her now. She had forgotten how wonderful it felt to give in to a man. To be absorbed in his smell, his taste, his strength. *Why was I fighting this?* She relaxed her jaw to let his tongue plunge inside as deep as he wanted.

His hands moved all over, from her hair to her breasts to her thighs. She shuddered when he parted her knees, as if she was surprised. He changed course and went back up to her breasts, cupping one of them as he pulled her closer with his other arm.

They continued to kiss as Victor undid her top button, then the next, giving his hand enough space to move into her blouse.

"Oh!" She gasped when she felt his fingers graze her hard nipple.

He broke the kiss. His lips went to her ear. "I'm sorry if I'm moving too fast. I can't help it. You drive me crazy."

"It's okay," she whispered in a breath.

"Good." Victor's mouth met hers again for a brief moment, then moved to her neck.

Cara's head fell backwards to give him room. His lips lingered there until she moaned, "Yes." He kissed her collarbone, then kissed further down until his mouth replaced his hand on her breast.

"Oh!" She didn't realize he had maneuvered her nipple out of her bra until she felt his soft lips against her skin, followed by the gentlest bite as he took her hard peak in between his teeth. "Oh my God!"

Inside, Victor smiled at her cry of pleasure. His longing mouth savored her plump breast as he undid another button.

Cara did her best to stifle the pleas that wanted to leave her throat. Victor had awakened feelings she forgot her body was capable of. Suddenly she wanted him everywhere. On top of her, inside of her. It no longer mattered if someone might hear.

And then, his hand slid across the slippery material covering her stomach.

"Oh no." She gritted her teeth.

Victor's mouth let go of her breast. He chuckled. "What the hell's this thing? A girdle?"

"I prefer the term 'body shaper.'"

He groaned. "I swear, you women. You don't need this thing, Cara."

She let out a tiny whine. "Yes, I do."

"No, you don't." He lifted his head to look in her eyes. "And to think, you wore this, knowing I was going to get you naked today?"

She gulped. Her voice was soft. "Well…I didn't…*know*…exactly…"

He sighed. "Is it okay if I peel you out of it?"

Cara stammered, suddenly feeling very much on display. "Um…I don't know…"

Victor grinned. "It's okay. It'll be my bedtime project.

Releasing you from this horribly constrictive device." With his eyes fixed on hers, he moved his hand down to her knee and quickly made his way up her skirt to cup her heat.

"Ooh!" Cara bit her lip and closed her eyes, now remembering how good it felt to have a man touch her there.

"Relax, *querida*," he whispered. He pulled a latch on the side of her chair, slowly leaning her backward until she was lying down.

Cara opened her eyes and stared straight up at the ceiling as he pushed her skirt all the way up to her waist and pried her knees apart, wide. Her eyes stayed on the ceiling. She was afraid if she looked at him, she would wake up and realize it had all been a daydream.

His fingers went back and forth across the fabric between her legs. "How does this thing work? Are these snaps?"

She winced with embarrassment. "Yes."

He chuckled. "Well, this should give me some easy access then, shouldn't it?"

In seconds he unfastened the three snaps that secured her undergarment, then pried them apart. "Mmm," he said. "I'm glad you're wearing nothing underneath. I was afraid there might be another barricade."

When she felt his gentle finger trail through her wetness, she let out a moan and spread her legs further, welcoming the man who was more of a stranger than a boss. For so long, she had every reason to resist any man who wanted her like this. And now, all she could think about was letting him inhabit every part of her. "Please, take me…"

Victor's fingers were soft at first but then grew urgent as he obeyed her breathy response.

"More, yes. More."

The words were quiet, barely escaping her mouth like she had no power to stop them. The more she moaned, the faster his fingers went. It had not been his intention to be so intimate so quickly, but he couldn't help himself. Not after feeling the need pooling between her thighs, and the way her hips moved against his hand as he rubbed her faster.

Victor fought the urge to use his tongue, choosing instead to save that for later tonight at the hotel. For now he was more than happy to watch the passion on her lovely face as his fingers moved faster and harder to please her.

When he sensed she was nearing climax, he dipped his fingers inside her.

"Yes!" she shouted.

He kept his fingers there and used his other hand to rub her tiny nub.

"Oh yes!" Cara bit her lip to try to keep herself from screaming, but her attempt was unsuccessful. She was no match for those skilled hands of his. Her sounds filled the tiny plane as her climax overtook her.

He reached inside his pocket for his wallet and quickly retrieved a condom.

She tilted her head up just enough to watch him unzip his pants, then unroll the condom down his shaft. Smiling, she let her head fall back into place against the padded seat.

Victor cradled a hand under each of her thighs to position himself perfectly.

"Is it okay if I do this?" His firm head was at her opening, begging for entrance.

As soon as she said, "Yes," he plunged inside and stayed there, still, until she opened her eyes to look at him.

"Cara," he said, "I didn't expect us to move so quickly, I swear."

"It's okay." She smiled. "I want this."

He nodded and whispered, "I want *you*."

Victor cradled her thighs as he moved between her legs, meeting her soft flesh over and over until his release many minutes later.

When he finished, he reached for her arms and said, "Sit up, *querida*."

She sat up. He was still perched between her legs on his knees.

He put his arms around her and kissed her, his hands roaming her back and her hair.

She met his kiss with passion, now completely unashamed that she was half naked and still wearing her body shaper. She tightened her knees against his hips as her hands roamed his back.

When he pulled away, he whispered in her ear, "You're so beautiful."

Breathing heavily, she whispered, "Thank you." She stopped herself before telling him she now realized just how much she needed what he had given her.

Several minutes later, after collecting themselves, Victor sat beside her and draped an arm around her shoulders. "So, let me guess what you're thinking." He cocked a brow. "You can't believe you just did that with your boss."

"Wow. You're a real mind reader." She smirked, then chuckled softly.

He sighed. "If it helps, I can't believe I just did that with an employee." He rubbed her shoulder. "But I don't regret it. Not for a second."

"Good." She nestled against his chest. "Neither do I. At least, not yet…"

"What's that supposed to mean?"

Cara took a deep breath and sat up straight, slightly away from him. "I still don't understand what's going on here. And maybe I never will."

"Don't question it. Just let yourself enjoy it."

"That's exactly what I'm trying to do." She hesitated for a moment, then added, "But, for the record, I want you to know that I don't exactly enjoy being a pawn in anyone's game."

Victor's face scrunched up in a bewildered expression. "Wait a minute. Who said you're a pawn?" He put one finger under her chin and turned her face to his, looking deeply into her eyes. "I already told you, I don't play games."

"Then what am I supposed to think about all this? I know we've already had this conversation but after what just happened, I think maybe it bears repeating—"

He placed two fingers against her lips. "No. When I want something, I'm not shy about it. And I want you, Cara."

She waited until he took his hand away. "Just tell me once and for all. Is this because of Alexis?"

He let out an exasperated groan. "Please don't mention her name to me again. Besides, how does me sleeping with you have anything to do with her?" He shrugged and glanced randomly around the plane. "Is she here, hiding somewhere, listening to us? Do you think I'm going to call her and tell her what we did? Do you think there's a hidden camera and she's watching from somewhere on the ground?"

"Oh God, I hope not."

He laughed heartily for a long moment. "No, there's none of that. How would any of this affect her? If I were trying to make her jealous I could do that without taking advantage of you on a private plane." Under his breath he muttered, "I already know she's jealous. She saw us at lunch last week. Gary told me she called the office."

"Should I be scared of her?"

He blew a scoffing breath out of the side of his mouth. "No. Absolutely not. If she ever contacts you, let me know. She has nothing to do with Monarch Enterprises and there should never be a reason for her to even come inside the office, unless it's another attempt to torment me like she did at the dinner."

"The dinner?"

"Yes, the charity dinner. Where I met you."

"Oh."

"I told you, I wasn't there with her. She planned that all by herself." He shook his head. "I was so pissed off about it that night. She just wanted everyone to talk about us and think we were back together."

"Why did you break up? It wasn't that long ago, was it?"

Victor sighed. "I'd rather not go into detail. Suffice it to say, I'm glad it's over. We were never right for each other."

"Then why were you with her, at all?"

He shrugged. "I don't know. It seemed perfect when we got together. And on paper, it truly *was* perfect. I'd spent so much of my youth working hard, busy trying to make something of myself. I guess I was afraid life would pass me by and I'd forget to settle down and have a family. Getting married was always on my list of things to do before I turned thirty, and I'm thirty-one now."

"You say 'thirty' like it's so old."

"I don't mean it that way. It's just that, time goes by way too fast. If you're not careful you can let years go by without accomplishing any of the things you thought you'd accomplish. That's my biggest fear. That I'll wake up one day and wonder where it all went. When I die, I won't be taking my investments or my penthouse or my sports car with me." He stared off thoughtfully at a window. "I want to leave a legacy."

Cara was taken aback. *Perhaps he is much deeper than I gave him credit for.* "And you couldn't have that legacy with her?"

He shook his head as if startled out of a trance. "No. She and I have very different priorities." Victor turned to her with a wry smile, to ask about something he had been waiting for some time to approach. "So, let's talk about your personal life for a while, Miss Green. Where's Isaac's father? Is he in the picture, at all?"

"I don't…" Cara's voice trailed off. A nagging feeling in the pit of her stomach would not permit her to use the lie she had given everyone since the day she announced her pregnancy. Maybe it was the hint of vulnerability Victor had shown that made her feel bad about lying to him. She knew she could not evade this issue for much longer, given the eagerness of Victor's tone. She swallowed hard and took another second to get her words in order. "No, he's not in the picture and he never will be."

"Is that by his choice, or yours?"

"Darn, you're really nosy."

"Just curious. You don't have to tell me, but…" He gave her shoulder a soft squeeze. "I'd kinda like to know. Isaac's a great kid. I hope to get to know him better. Get to know you both better, if that's okay."

Cara gulped. This was not what she had expected, at all. "Um…I don't know what to say except, Isaac's father is not a concern."

"Good."

Her eyebrows furrowed. "And I don't let Isaac get attached to people. He needs stability."

Victor held her gaze for a moment, then looked down at the floor. "I understand that. You're a good mother. Has that happened before? You dated someone and Isaac got his heart broken?"

"Uh…are we dating? Is that what you call this?"

With a half-hearted shrug, he said, "I don't know. I wouldn't say we're *not* dating. So, tell me. Did Isaac get attached to someone?"

A chaotic swirl of thoughts entered Cara's mind. Too rattled to consider her options, she said, "No, he's never gotten attached to anyone, not like a father."

Victor's eyebrows knitted. "You've dated since he was born, haven't you?"

Her voice was weak. "No. Not really."

"Not really?"

She cleared her throat. "Not at all, actually."

Victor's eyes were huge. "Okay. Let me ask something else…before today, when's the last time you slept with a man?"

A thin layer of tears suddenly clouded her vision. "It was Isaac's father."

"Oh." Victor's eyebrows rose. "Wow. I didn't know. I'm sorry —"

She held up her hand. "Don't." She sniffled. "Please don't be sorry. I didn't plan for it to happen that way." She wiped her hand across her face to erase the few drops that rolled down her cheek. "I guess it's a lot like what you said about time going by. Wondering where it went. I get that. This wasn't how I planned it. I didn't know I'd give so much to my career only to have it taken away so I could move back home."

Victor gave her a knowing smile. "It's almost useless to plan. I can't tell you how many times I've thought I had everything all worked out and then…boom. My world turns upside down." He sighed. "I guess that's why I got engaged. I wanted something permanent in my life, besides work. Wanted a sure thing."

Cara wiped her face again, nodding. "The only sure thing to me is Isaac. He's the true love of my life."

"I understand." Victor tightened his grip around her shoulders. "You have every right to be protective." Gently, he placed his hand on top of hers. "But I'd really love to get to know both of you better. I hope you'll let me."

Cara's voice trembled. "Maybe."

"I know you just met me. You don't have to give me an answer right now." He kissed her forehead. "Just let things take their natural course."

She nodded. "Okay."

In a deadpan voice, he added, "And please don't file sexual harassment charges against me."

She laughed, grateful he had added some levity to their conversation. "I wasn't planning to."

"Good." He grinned. "Because technically, it's not harassment as far as I know. I never said you had to sleep with me to get a job or get promoted. I waited over a week after your date of employment before I got you on a private jet alone and coerced you to be my lover."

Cara laughed. "It didn't take much coercion."

He narrowed his eyes, nodding. "It took a lot more than you realize. You're a stubborn woman." He kissed her cheek. "And now I have to figure out a way to focus on those stuffed shirts at the Lochmere Group for an entire afternoon until we can be alone again." He sighed. "You have no idea the effect you have on me."

Cara wiped away the last of her tears. "How much longer till we land?"

Victor looked at his wristwatch. "Another hour."

"Should we go over the Lochmere file again?"

"Nah." Victor drew her into a deep kiss, his thoughts consumed with something else he wanted to do again before they landed.

CHAPTER TEN

Alexis signaled to Tom as she sipped her martini.

It took Tom a few seconds to see the redhead at the bar, snapping her fingers high in the air. He nodded and rushed toward her, feeling very out of place in this hoity toity midtown bar.

"Ms. Whitt." He extended his hand. "Good to see you again."

"Yes." Alexis shook his hand. "Thank you for meeting me here."

Tom straightened his glasses. "All part of the job, ma'am."

"Have a seat." She patted the bar stool next to her. "Drinks are on me."

He chuckled to himself and asked the bartender for a scotch on the rocks. When he retired from the police force two years earlier, he had no idea he would end up tracking down ex-lovers of spoiled socialites. The guys at the station would have a good laugh if they ever found out about it. "Care to move to a table or you wanna do this at the bar?"

"Bar's fine." Alexis took a long sip of her drink. "Please don't drag it out. Just give me the bad news."

"As you wish." He pulled his phone and a small notebook out of his pocket. "The girl's name is Cara Green. She's a single mom who lives on Brockton Avenue in Newark with her widowed mother."

Alexis's mouth dropped open. She swiveled on her stool to face him. "Single mom? Newark? Are you sure?"

"Absolutely." He handed her his camera. "He went to her house for dinner on Friday night."

Alexis scrolled through the pictures. "Is this the kid?" Her eyes grew wider with every photo of the tiny boy sitting in Victor's car, holding the steering wheel. "Has this been going on for a long time?"

"Dunno, ma'am."

"It had to be. They look like they've known each other for a while." Alexis let out a sound of disgust when she came to the pictures of Cara joining them outside. "What does he see in this woman?"

Tom silently took a sip of the scotch that had just appeared in front of him.

"Is it the kid?" Alexis asked. "Is that what he wants? Is that why he won't get back together with me?"

"I can try to find out."

"Did he father this child or something? Was he living a double life I never knew about?"

"Couldn't tell ya ma'am. But I can dig deeper if ya want."

"Sure, sure." Alexis waved her hand dismissively. "Whatever. Money's no object. Find out about this kid's paternity." She sighed. "If nothing else, maybe I can make *her* ex really jealous with some pictures. That'd break 'em up, for sure."

Tom took another drink. "I'll do my best. Oh, almost forgot. She lost her job in Chicago about six months ago. That's how she ended up back home in Newark. Probably needed her mother to take care of the boy. Day care's expensive and—"

Alexis shook her head. "Whatever. I need to get her away from him. I don't care what it takes. Jealous baby daddy. Or maybe find some way to get her to move back to Chicago." She emptied her martini into her mouth and swallowed. "You came highly recommended, Tom. Please live up to my expectations."

Tom sighed. He could get her the information she desired, but he was convinced it would do nothing to help her win her fiance back. "I said I'll do my best, ma'am." He looked at his watch. "It's noon. If I head out now, I might have some more information for you today."

"Great." Alexis choked back her tears.

* * *

"Isaac, be careful on that swing," Patty called out.

Isaac waved at his grandmother then threw his head back, laughing, as his new friend Alissa pushed him higher.

Feeling a chill in the air, Patty pulled her sweater across her chest a little tighter and relaxed against the steel bench.

A portly gray-haired man with a newspaper in his hand sat down beside her. "I knew I wasn't the only one who felt a nip in the air."

Patty raised one eyebrow, nodding slowly. "Oh yes. I can tell we're gonna have an early winter this year."

He smiled. "I've been thinking the same thing all day."

Patty narrowed her eyes. "Have I seen you here before? You don't look familiar. I thought I knew all the grandfathers in the neighborhood."

"No, we've never met." He held out his hand. "Tom Sutton. Nice to meet you."

Patty shook his hand. "Likewise, Mr. Sutton. Patty Green."

"Please, call me Tom."

"Call me Patty." She grinned. "So, is one of these rug rats yours?"

"No." Tom glanced around at the small mass of children playing in front of them. "I have four grandkids, all in Connecticut. Today I'm just out and about. Went to a deli around the corner. Thought I'd stop by the park and read the newspaper for a while." He turned to her. "One of these yours?"

"Yes." She pointed. "Fluffy hair, blue-striped shirt. Laughing his head off on the swings."

"I see." Tom straightened his glasses, feeling a twinge of guilt that he already knew what Isaac Green looked like. He took a deep breath and went on, determined to do the job he was paid to do. "He looks like a handful."

"He is." She sighed as she watched him. "He certainly is. But I don't know what I'd do without him now. He and his mother moved in with me a while back." She turned to Tom, shrugging. "Recession casualty. My daughter had a great job in Chicago. Then one day." She drew her hand across her neck in a line. "Axed."

"Sorry to hear it."

"S'okay. She finally got another job. Started last week."

"Good for her. Here in Newark?"

"No, it's some ritzy place in Manhattan."

This is going to be easier than I thought. Tom asked, "So, how'd she get a job like that? I know people who been outta work for a year or more. She know someone?"

Patty kept one eye on Isaac to make sure he was okay. "Sorta. She met a guy when she was working at a catering job for all these rich people. Next thing I know, she's getting all dressed up and driving to Manhattan every morning." She sighed. "I figure she'll get 'em an apartment there, soon as she finds one she can afford. The drive every day is starting to get to her."

"I would imagine so. I never drive there unless I absolutely have to."

"Me neither." Patty shrugged. "But she hates the train."

"So, you're the full time babysitter? Your daughter divorced or something?"

Patty shook her head. "No, Isaac's never had a father. A one night stand in college. Isaac's our little souvenir, courtesy Drexel University."

Tom let out a nervous chuckle. "These kids these days, I tell ya. They do anything with anyone."

"Well, my Cara's not a slut. I can promise you that."

"I'm so sorry. I didn't mean to imply such a thing. I was just saying—"

"No, no. You're right. These kids. But my Cara isn't like that." She patted his knee. "So, what about you? What's your story?"

"Oh, there's not much to tell. I'm a widower. Retired cop."

"Cop?" Patty's eyes perked up. "My Nathan was a cop. Killed in the line of duty eleven years ago next month."

Tom put his hand over his heart, then gave her a reassuring tap on the arm. "I'm so sorry. Truly sorry. Was it here in Newark?"

"Yep."

"And you stayed in the area?"

"Yep. Makes me feel closer to him. What about you? Where'd you work?"

"Brooklyn."

"Oh. I bet your wife was pacing the floor every night until you walked in the door."

"Yes." Tom nodded. "And I heard about it every single day."

"And you're a widower, you said?"

"Yes. Breast cancer." He let out a sad sigh. "Happened quickly, almost three years ago."

Patty gave Isaac a quick glance then rested her hand on Tom's knee, angling her body to fully face him. "I'm so sorry."

"Yeah. It was rough, but I've got a lot to be thankful for." He gave her a warm grin and reached into his pocket to turn off his recording device. "So, are you familiar with Bryson's Deli a few blocks from here? They make the best cannoli."

"Oh, no. You've never tried my cannoli. In fact, I was just thinking I hadn't made those in a while. You like Italian food?"

"Do I ever?" Tom put his newspaper down on the bench. This new assignment of his was starting to feel a lot less grueling.

* * *

"Great work today." Victor squeezed Cara's hand as they walked into the restaurant.

"Thanks."

It was seven o'clock in the evening and instead of being alone in a hotel room, Victor had whisked her off to a restaurant. She smiled, trying to hide her disappointment as she watched him speak to the hostess. When he finished, Cara said, "So, you still haven't told me who we're meeting for dinner. Is it one of the guys from Lochmere?"

Victor glanced at his phone again. "No. We're meeting my brother, Ramon."

Cara's eyes widened. "What?"

Victor laughed. "Don't be scared."

"I'm not scared, I'm surprised. Why didn't you tell me this earlier?"

"Because it took me two days to get up with him, and then I wasn't sure he could get here. He runs a ranch about three hours away, near San Antonio. I try to see him if I happen to be in Texas but he can't always get away on short notice."

"Your brother owns a ranch?"

"Yes. It's the same ranch where we all worked when we left Mexico."

"So, he moved there and never left the ranch?"

Victor laughed. "It's funny to hear you put it that way. But yes, that's essentially what happened. I went off to college, and Armando followed my lead a few years later. But Ramon always knew that wasn't for him. He liked the outdoors, the hard physical labor. But these days he oversees that ranch and two others." He shook his head. "I don't know how he does it. He's not outside in the fresh air nearly as much these days but he puts in more hours than ever."

Cara examined Victor from head to toe. He was so polished in his black fitted suit, it was hard to imagine him working as a ranch hand. Cara asked, "So, what does Armando do for a living?"

With a light shrug, Victor said, "Same thing as me, mostly. Asset management, helping venture capitalists find new investments. But he's in Los Angeles."

"Do you see your brothers very often?"

He let out a sad sigh. "Not nearly as often as I'd like."

Just then, Victor turned around in the direction of a surprise slap on his shoulder. His face lit up when he saw Ramon.

Cara watched as they hugged. Ramon was as handsome as Victor, but his face was obviously a little more weathered from being outdoors in the hot Texas sun.

Ramon put his arm around Victor. "Leave it to you to pick some ritzy restaurant like this. Make me wear a suit."

Victor smirked. "It's good for you once in a while."

Ramon peered down at his dark gray ensemble. "Can you see the dust on this thing?" He sighed and gave Victor's back a hearty slap, then extended his hand to Cara. "Hello there. My name is Ramon Barboza. Please forgive my rude brother for not introducing us himself."

Victor elbowed him. "You didn't give me time." He motioned to Cara. "Cara, my brother, Ramon." He looked at Ramon and gestured to Cara. "Ramon, Cara Green."

Cara felt the rough skin on Ramon's hand as she shook it. "Nice to meet you."

"Nice to meet you as well." Ramon smiled and gave her hand a quick shake then turned to his brother. "So, co-worker? Girlfriend?"

Victor's eyes narrowed at him as he considered his response.

Cara spoke up. "We just started working together last week."

Ramon nodded and shot Victor a sly glance. "And yet, he brought you with him to meet his brother. That sounds pretty serious."

Victor knew his youngest brother too well. Ramon wanted to embarrass him. It wasn't malicious. It was just Ramon's way. "It's none of your business." He smiled. "Now that you're here I'll tell the hostess we're ready for our table."

As they trailed behind the hostess and Ramon to their table, Victor took Cara's arm and whispered in her ear, "Just so you know, I was going to say you were my girlfriend."

Cara blushed and tucked her head down to hide her smile.

Soon they were seated around a small round table in the bustling restaurant.

Victor quietly nudged Cara as Ramon placed his drink order. "Order something that'll make you crazy for me later. But pace yourself. I definitely need you awake."

Cara giggled. "I'll see what I can do." When the waitress

came to her, Cara ordered a rum and coke.

Victor thought about telling Cara how nice it was to see her so relaxed, even without the assistance of alcohol. But he was afraid it would appeal to her stubbornness, causing her to rebel and put her guard up. The wiser choice was to stay quiet.

After the waitress left, Victor said, "So how's business? You turning a good profit this quarter?"

Ramon nodded. "Looks that way. Best quarter since 2007. Seems like business is finally turning around."

"Great," Victor said. "I was starting to get worried."

Ramon cocked an eyebrow. "There's no reason to worry about me. You know I always have a handle on things. You still planning to come down and visit before the end of the year?"

"Yes." Victor nodded.

Ramon smiled. "You gonna bring Cara when you come? I'm sure she'd love it."

Determined not to let Ramon embarrass him again, Victor offered a casual shrug and said, "Maybe. Cara actually has a little boy who'd probably love to make a mess of himself there."

Cara nodded. "He loves animals. He rode a pony at a birthday party a few months ago and it was all he talked about for days."

Ramon chuckled. "How old is he?"

"Three, almost three and a half," Cara said.

Victor said, "He's really cute. And really smart."

"Thanks." Cara grinned.

"So, are you divorced?" Ramon asked.

Cara quickly shook her head. "No. Never married."

Ramon nodded. "Does the father live around you? Joint custody?"

Victor let out a loud sigh of displeasure, although he secretly wanted to know how she would answer. "Cara, please forgive my nosy brother."

Cara gulped. "It's okay. Isaac's dad isn't around, at all."

Ramon said, "I'm sorry. Didn't mean to pry. Always curious about that. Did Victor tell you we grew up without a dad?"

Cara nodded. "Yes. He mentioned that."

"There was Mr. Platt," Victor said. "Henry Platt. He's the benefactor who moved us to Texas when we were kids. He was like a father."

Cara noticed Ramon's face darken at the mention of Henry Platt. Hesitantly, she asked a question. "It's really nice that you had such a generous benefactor. I don't think I've ever heard of anything like that before."

Victor and Ramon both nodded.

"Yes," Victor said. "It was like winning the lottery. I don't know where we would be without him." He sighed. "I tried to call him to say I was in the area but I got a message saying he's out of town. It was kind of weird. You know what that's about?"

Ramon shrugged. "He's the same old asshole he always was. That's what it's about."

Victor glared at Ramon. "Come on, now. Whatever differences you've had, he doesn't deserve that."

The drinks came right then and Ramon immediately brought his to his lips, ignoring Victor's rebuke.

An hour later, they were almost finished with their entrees. Ramon plied Cara with stories of their upbringing, most of them making Victor laugh. Some made his cheeks turn pink.

After Cara's third rum and coke she excused herself to go to the ladies' room.

"So." Ramon put his elbows on the table, leaning forward. "You're dating a girl who has a kid?"

"What's wrong with that?" Victor asked.

"Nothing. Just never knew you to do that before. Sounds like you just met her and you're already pretty serious."

Victor wiped his mouth with his napkin then placed it on the table. "It seems to be heading in that direction. At least, I hope it is."

"Be careful. You date a girl like that, you're dating the kid, too."

"I've considered that very carefully and I've decided I like the idea." Victor picked up his water. "I'm not sure if Cara's too keen on the idea but she seems to be warming up to it."

"She looked a little weird when I asked about the father, don't you think?"

Victor shrugged. "Could've just been because a stranger asked her a question that was pretty damn intrusive."

"Yeah, maybe," Ramon said. "You ever think about our father?"

"What's there to think about? We never knew him."

"Hmm. You still believe that?"

"Ah, Ramon." Victor frowned. "You and your conspiracy theories." He looked up as he saw Cara reenter the room. "Here she comes."

Ramon smiled as he watched his brother's face light up, and his eyes follow his new love interest through the room. Ramon had long ago forgotten how it felt to be jealous of his brother, until tonight.

CHAPTER ELEVEN

"So, your brother's single?" Cara asked as she snuggled up to Victor on the elevator. They were in their hotel, on the way to their rooms.

"Why? You're not interested, are you?"

"No."

"Good." He kissed her forehead. "Why do you ask?"

"My best friend Marcy's single."

Victor produced a sarcastic laugh. "Unless she's willing to move to a five thousand acre ranch in Texas, there's no reason to try. Ramon may be younger than me but he's pretty set in his ways. Any woman who'll take him on will have to accommodate him, trust me."

It's a good thing Marcy loves a challenge, Cara thought, grinning. "So, do you miss the ranch? You spoke of it so fondly."

"I have good memories there and it will always be a very special place to me. But I wouldn't say I miss it. I like living in the city."

"Were you serious about taking me and Isaac there to visit?"

"Maybe." He smiled. "We'll see what happens, I guess."

The elevator stopped at their floor. Victor took Cara's hand and led her into the hallway, then to the rooms they reserved for the night.

They stood hand in hand, staring at the two doors.

"So." Cara gulped. "Is this where we part ways?"

Victor looked at her like she was crazy. "Are you kidding me? How many times today have I told you what I wanna do to you when I get you alone in the hotel?"

"Then why'd we get two rooms? I don't understand."

"Oh, silly girl. It's all for show. The ladies in accounting would have a field day if they saw the expense reports for this trip and there's only one hotel room."

Cara let out the breath she didn't realize she had been holding. "Okay. I probably should've realized that. I feel so stupid now."

"You're not stupid, Cara."

"I think maybe I was just afraid to get my hopes up. I didn't know if our night together was a sure thing or not."

Victor threw his head back with a gentle laugh, then put his hands on her face. "*Mi querida*, tonight is definitely a sure thing."

With that, he overtook her mouth with a hard kiss. One that he had fantasized about giving her for hours. Several times today he had taken a private moment to kiss her, but not like this. It was almost time to take her to bed where he could have her and be completely unrestrained. Give in to his urges.

When he pulled away, he stroked her cheek and said, "Let's get your luggage out of your room now and put it in mine."

Cara shyly bit her lip. "Actually, do you think I could go to my room and freshen up for a minute? I just want everything to be perfect."

"Hmm." Victor thought about it for a second. "Fine. Whatever makes you comfortable. But I have a request."

"Okay…"

"There should be a robe in your closet, compliments of the hotel. Wear it." He gave her lips a light kiss. "And nothing else."

Cara's eyes grew wide. "Nothing else?"

"No," he whispered. "Now go in there and get ready. I'll knock on your door in fifteen minutes. Does that give you enough time?"

Cara swallowed, hard. "Yeah. I think so."

"Good." He kissed her once more then reached into his pocket for his key card. "Now, hurry. I'll be there in fifteen minutes. And I'm always prompt." He flashed one last smile then disappeared into his room.

Nervous, Cara fumbled in her purse for the key. *Naked? Completely naked? Hopefully we can leave the lights off.*

Ten minutes later, Cara was drying herself off after the quickest shower of her lifetime. She used the complimentary hair dryer to dry the wispy hairs that had gotten damp in spite of her shower cap.

She took several deep breaths to calm herself down. She wanted this, there was no question about it. Being with him again was all she could think about after their encounter on the plane earlier today. Maybe it was the surprise of it all, or the fact that she was still mostly clothed at the time, but now she felt a million times more vulnerable. Tonight, she was the object of his desire, and she knew it. The thought of it filled her with a mix of emotions ranging from elation to dread. Hopefully once she was in his arms again, the dread would disappear. Victor had made her feel beautiful today. Who was she to tell him he was wrong?

Five minutes later, after brushing her teeth and spritzing herself with just the right amount of perfume, she heard a knock at the door.

She took another deep breath then opened the closet door and reached for the robe. She quickly slipped it on and tightened the belt around her waist, tying a loose knot.

Cara turned off the light switch and pulled the door open.

"Hello there," she said.

Victor unconsciously licked his lips when he saw her. He had left his jacket and tie in his room. His shirt was unbuttoned, exposing the thin T-shirt he wore underneath.

He put his arms around her back and kissed her as he walked her backward into the room until the door slammed shut. Then he pulled away. "Wait. It's too dark in here."

"No it's not. There's plenty of light coming in from outside. The moon's almost full."

"No, no, no. Don't be one of those women, Cara. I wanna see the beautiful body I'm about to make love to."

Cara tried to grin as warmth rushed to her cheeks. "That's really sweet. But I don't feel comfortable with the lights on."

"But I've been looking forward to this. I suppose we'll have to compromise." With a sigh, he let her go and walked to the desk. "Here. A desk lamp. Perfect."

Suddenly, the small light came on and the room was brighter.

"See?" he said. "It's dim enough for you and bright enough for me."

"I don't know..."

"Cara." He came up to her and put his arms around her, his hands sliding down to her butt where he grabbed a chunk in each hand. "I can't wait to see what's under that robe. Believe me, I won't be disappointed."

Cara swooned for a moment, then caught herself. "I hope you're right about that."

With a resigned sigh, he let go of her and sat at the foot of the bed. "All right," he said. "Now take off the robe."

Every nerve in her body tightened with fear. She could only stare down at the floor, unable to speak.

"Cara." He softened his voice. "Please. Take it off. I've waited so long—"

Her voice was weak. "That's not true. We've only known each other a few weeks."

"Fine. Maybe it just feels like that long because I've thought about you so much. Come on, *querida*." He looked in her eyes with a pained expression. "Please, give me this."

"I can't…"

"Yes, you can. One step at a time. First, untie the belt…"

The first guy I've slept with in four years wants to see me naked? I should've asked to bring a bottle of rum back to my room. She closed her eyes and did as he requested, slowly untying the belt at her waist and letting the ends dangle at her sides.

"Good." Victor grinned. "Now take each side of the robe and pull it away from your body. Start with the right side, then the left."

It had to be done. There was no getting out of it, not now. She took a slow breath, closed her eyes, and opened the right side of the robe, then the left, as he instructed. A draft of air hit her naked flesh, making her shiver.

An uncontrollable, eager moan escaped Victor's throat. He said, "Come here."

She opened her eyes just enough to see her way to the bed where he sat, shuffling along until her knees touched his.

He reached around her, hands sliding under the robe to the

backs of her thighs, holding her steady as he whispered, "I don't know what you're so worried about." He lightly kissed her stomach, nearly making her giggle. "I'm so glad you're mine tonight."

Cara cried out in pleasure and went weak at her knees when she felt the warmth of his lips around her breast. When his tongue circled her nipple, her mouth dropped open and she grabbed the back of his head, holding him there. "Yes…yes."

Victor spent a while there, losing himself in the fullness of her breasts. His hands slowly crept up her back until they arrived near her shoulders. Then he stood up, kissing her lips to distract her while he gently pulled at the arms of the robe.

She was too wrapped up in his kiss to realize her only covering had fallen to the floor behind her. When she shivered, he pulled her closer, crushing her in a tight embrace to keep her warm.

Seconds later, he surprised her by spinning her around to the bed. She had barely let out a gasp when he hovered over her on his elbows, letting his body weight rest lightly on top of her.

Victor nibbled her ear, then her neck.

Cara whispered, "Why am I the only one naked?"

He let out a playful moan. "Because I'm your boss and I want you that way." He kissed her again before she could respond. As his tongue worked inside her mouth, he reached down between their bodies to part her legs. His fingers were bold, stroking her where she was wet and swollen.

Cara's thoughts about her own body were completely replaced by thoughts about Victor's. His fingers, his tongue. The erection she could feel, rubbing against her bare thigh. She reached down to cup him through the outside of his pants but he immediately pushed her hand away.

"Not yet. I must do something else first." He sat up and launched himself off the bed.

"What are you doing?" A chill passed through her. She already missed the warmth of his body lying against hers.

"Don't worry. I can warm you much better from down here." Victor bent forward and slid his hands under her thighs, pulling her to the edge of the bed. Then he knelt on the floor.

Cara felt his tongue against her lower lips before her mind could process what he meant. Never had such intense pleasure flooded her being so quickly. There was nothing else left in her world…only the feel of his tongue. She shrieked and moaned. Her body writhed against him in an uncontrollable rhythm, but his firm grip under her knees held her just where he wanted her.

What he said about warming her was absolutely true. She was so hot now, she imagined herself melting right through the mattress. His tongue was everywhere at once, touching her in ways she forgot existed. Her entire body trembled with each lick until her mouth opened wide, filling the room with the sounds of her climax.

As Cara lay still, recovering, Victor stood up.

He wiped his mouth against his long sleeve then reached inside his pocket for a condom. His eyes went up and down her body, devouring her as he undressed. He felt like he couldn't get his clothes off fast enough.

Cara had finally caught her breath when she opened her eyes and saw Victor, naked, unrolling the condom. The sight renewed her energy. His body was tight and athletic. His chest, smooth and perfectly toned. She smiled up at him when he pulled her legs apart a little more and leaned forward.

Victor intertwined his fingers with hers and held her hands down on the bed as he slipped inside of her.

Her head fell back as she cried out in ecstasy. The louder she got, the faster he went, driving himself deeper into her.

He waited for her eyes to meet his. He could barely breathe as he said, "You're so beautiful, Cara."

She could only stare up at him, mesmerized. Watching his face grow more and more intense with each stroke until he closed his eyes, grunting and gritting his teeth as he came.

Victor soon lay alongside her, catching his breath. "Ohhh… Cara…" He took a deep breath. "Please…forgive me…"

"Forgive you?" Her eyebrows furrowed as she watched his face. "For what?"

Another deep breath. "For rushing you…into bed…couldn't help myself…so beautiful…"

Cara was again rendered speechless, wondering momentarily if Victor was a figment of her imagination. She had never felt more desired in her entire life. Letting his words sink in, she waited for his breathing to return to normal, then she said, "You didn't rush me, Victor. I wanted this to happen."

He brushed a lock of her hair behind her ear. "Good. I know it's fast. And I meant what I said on the plane today. I really do want to get to know you better." He gave her a lopsided smile. "But you're just too damn tempting." He cupped her cheek. "Too damn sexy."

Instantly, Victor's hand slid to her hair, pulling her face to his for a kiss. He let her go for a second and said, "I don't know if I'm gonna get any sleep tonight,"

When his lips returned, Cara felt her body heat rise once again with the hope that neither of them would sleep.

CHAPTER TWELVE

Tom Sutton rubbed his eyes and looked up at the unfamiliar ceiling overhead. He was alone in bed, the smell of fresh coffee wafting in to keep him company.

He sat up, ready to go downstairs to greet the lovely Patty when he heard the tapping of tiny feet outside the door.

"Gwammah?" Isaac knocked. "Gwammah you up?"

Tom winced. The last thing he wanted was to confuse the cute little guy by walking out of his grandma's bedroom first thing in the morning.

"Isaac!" Tom heard Patty's voice call up the stairs. "Is that you I hear? Go back to your room, sweetie. I have a surprise for you."

Isaac said, "Mommy up?"

Patty's voice sounded closer now. "No, sweetie, Mommy will be home tonight. Remember we talked about this?"

"No."

Patty sighed. "Yes you do. Mommy had to work last night."

Isaac whined and stomped his foot. "*Mommy!*"

"Shh," Patty said. "Look what I have for you. A cinnamon roll."

Isaac's tone was instantly happy. "*Ooh!*"

"Now, I'll give you this but you need to be good, okay? Here. Go back to your room and I'll be there in a minute."

A few seconds later, Patty opened her bedroom door. "Good morning, handsome," she said.

Tom chuckled. "Good morning, my dear."

"This is for you." She handed him a hot cinnamon roll on a small plate, with a fork. "I hope you like sweets for breakfast."

Tom took the plate. "I love them. How'd you sneak out of here and have time to do this?"

With an air of false humility, Patty brushed her hair off her shoulder and said, "A woman has her ways."

Tom thought back to recent memories of the previous night. "Yes. She sure does."

They shared a knowing look and burst into laughter until Tom realized Isaac might hear. Then he got quiet.

He gave Patty a kiss on the cheek. "I'm sorry. I'll have to eat and run. I don't want your grandson to catch me here."

"Oh, I can take care of him. Don't worry about that."

"I really do have to go. I'm sorry. I have some important business to take care of and it can't wait any longer. I wish it could." He let out a wistful sigh. "Oh, I wish it could."

Disappointed, Patty nodded and watched him get dressed. "I understand."

A few minutes later, Patty and Tom walked down to the front door, quickly joined by Isaac, who hid behind Patty's leg.

"Well, you have my number and you know where to find me," she said.

Tom looked down at Isaac to make sure he was not

watching, then kissed Patty's cheek. "I'd like to see you soon, if that's okay."

Patty beamed. "Dinner here tonight? You could meet my daughter."

A nervous twinge formed in Tom's stomach at the mention of Cara. "I'd like that."

"Seven o'clock then?"

"Yes." He kissed her cheek once more. "I'll be here."

An hour and a half later, Tom arrived at the usual meeting spot to speak with Alexis.

After sipping water at a table by himself for a few minutes, he watched the socialite waltz through the room, smiling.

Alexis sat across from him. "So, this must be important. I didn't expect to hear from you so soon." She rubbed her hands together. "So, let's get to it."

Tom folded his hands across the table. "Fine. There's no easy way to say this." He cleared his throat. "I can't work for you anymore."

"What? No!"

"Yes, Ms. Whitt. I'm off the case."

Alexis crossed her arms over her chest, pursing her lips. "You can't be off the case. We have a contract. I've already had money wired to your account."

Tom shrugged. "I'll unwire the money. Send it right back to you. Either of us can void that contract at any time."

Alexis fumed. She was more desperate than ever for new information, especially after hearing from another source that Cara and Victor went away on a business trip the previous day. "So, you have nothing new to tell me? I thought you were working this case all day yesterday."

Tom gave her a lighthearted grin and adjusted his glasses. "I was, indeed. But no more. I got no news for ya. I'm done."

Huffing loudly, Alexis spit out her words. "I'll ruin your name. You'll never work for anyone again if I have anything to do with it."

Tom took a deep breath and stood. "Well, you do what you gotta do, Ms. Whitt. I got some other business to attend to. Expect the money to be returned to your account in the next few days." And with that, he nodded one last time and walked out of the restaurant.

Cursing under her breath, Alexis took out her phone to make a call. "Hey, Sally?"

"Hey Alexis. Let me put you on hold for a sec." Sally, a staff accountant at Monarch Enterprises, waved for one of her co-workers to leave her cubicle, then returned to the phone. "So, what can I do for you today?"

"I just wanted to double check what you told me about Victor's trip request. His flight's scheduled to return at what time today?"

"Give me a moment to pull it up." Sally double-clicked on the travel module and entered Victor's name. "Hmm. He's traveled a lot lately. Okay, here's today's trip. He was originally supposed to return today at four o'clock. It can change at the last minute, though."

"Four o'clock?" Alexis's heart sank. "That means they've spent almost all day together."

"Sorry, hon. I can't do anything about that."

Alexis sighed. "I know. I'll talk to you later, okay? I gotta go."

Sally had barely said, "Goodbye," when Alexis ended the call.

Alexis hung her head, quietly crying in the middle of the crowded restaurant. It was time to plan her next move. She had no idea it would hurt so much to think Victor may have an interest in another woman. Whatever it took, she would get him back.

Men don't say, "no" to Alexis Whitt.

* * *

At five o'clock, Cara and Victor greeted Gary as they walked to Cara's office.

Victor waited for Cara to set her laptop bag down, then he shut the door behind them and pulled her into a kiss.

Cara never thought she would feel so comfortable kissing a man in the office, let alone her boss. But she came back from Houston with a new sense of confidence, ready to see where life would take her and Victor.

His tongue searched her mouth desperately until he absolutely had to pull away. "I'm sorry. I'll be late for a dinner meeting if I don't leave now. I'd ask you to join me but I've already kept you from Isaac for too long."

Cara nodded. "I understand."

"Please tell him Big Toe says hi." Victor laughed. "I'll call you tonight, hopefully not too late." He gave her another peck on the lips, then opened the door and left.

Cara walked to her chair and sat down, taking a moment to steady herself before docking her laptop to finish some work. Her life had never felt more like a whirlwind, and for once, she appreciated the sudden changes instead of doing everything in her power to stop them.

After she was settled in at her desk, she found her cell phone in her purse and dialed Marcy.

"*Cara?*" Marcy answered.

"Hey. How are you?"

Marcy let out a little gasp. "*Me? No, no, no. You better be calling to tell me all about what happened with Mr. Boss Man.*

Especially after that little text message you sent this morning."

Cara giggled and peered through her door to make sure Gary was busy at his desk. "I don't know where to start. He's amazing, Marcy."

"*Yeah, I'll bet. Did he show you some amazing moves last night?*"

"Shut up!" Cara felt her cheeks blush. "And yes."

Marcy cackled. "*It's about time! Details! I need details!*"

"Not now. I'm at work. You free to come over tonight?"

"*Maybe. Lost one of my offices today. Got swiped out from under me by some other cleaning crew.*"

"Oh, I'm so sorry…"

"*It's okay. I'll figure it out. So, back to you. Is it getting serious? Or is it just a sizzling hot work fling?*"

"I really don't know." Cara bit her fingernail. "He says we're dating."

"*Well, what do you say? Are you dating or not?*"

"Yeah. I suppose we are."

"*Good. I was gonna slap you if you said no to that.*"

Cara laughed for a moment. "But it's a little scary. He says if we don't work out he'll find me another job. How do I know he's telling me the truth?"

"*Stop freaking out. Just let it happen.*"

"I'm not freaking out. I'm a lot calmer than I sound." Cara sucked in a breath. "I remember what I wanted to tell you. He has a brother. Ramon."

"*Okay. A single brother?*"

"Yes."

"*So…you wanna introduce me?*"

"Maybe, but there's a slight catch. He lives in Texas."

"*Texas?*"

"Yes. He lives on a ranch."

"*Huh? A ranch? Like, with cows and stuff?*"

"Yes, with cows and stuff. It's the same ranch where Victor and his brothers grew up."

"*Huh.*" Marcy paused. "*Would he move to Jersey, you think?*"

"It's doubtful. But he's *so* gorgeous. Totally your type." Cara smiled as she imagined introducing the two. Marcy was a curvy, pretty brunette who seemed cursed with bad luck when it came to picking the right men. *Maybe she just needs someone else to do the picking*, Cara thought.

"*Hmm. Well, you never know.*" Marcy sighed. "*Let's work on you first, though.*"

"Okay. Just wanted to let you know about him. Hey, I probably better go. I have a few things to do before I leave."

"*See you tonight.*"

"Bye."

At five-thirty, Cara strolled through the parking garage, dangling her keys in her hand. As she approached her car, the door of a small Mercedes convertible opened two spaces away from her. Cara's neck tensed when she saw the woman who stepped out of it.

"Are you Cara?" Alexis asked.

Cara stopped in her tracks. "Excuse me?"

Alexis took off her sunglasses and slinked toward Cara, her stilettos clacking loudly across the pavement. She narrowed her eyes and looked Cara up and down. "Well, well, well. Victor must be slumming these days."

Cara put her fist on her hip. "Again. Excuse me?"

"You heard me." Alexis scoffed. "You don't really think you have a chance with him, do you? What man in his right mind would pick you over," she gestured to her small frame, wearing a tight blue dress, "this?"

Her jaw firmly set, Cara looked in her eyes. "He didn't seem to have a problem with it last night." She grinned. "Or this morning. Or yesterday—"

Alexis stepped forward. "Do you really think you can please a man like him? He's used to a different class of woman. A higher class."

"A higher class? You mean, the kind of woman who gets another woman fired just to assert her power?"

"You got yourself fired. You're the one who broke the rules with your cell phone that night."

Cara's jaw dropped. "Are you really that petty? You think I deserved to be fired because I took five seconds to find out if my son needed emergency surgery?"

Alexis shrugged. "Rules are rules. If he was sick, you should've been home with him. I'd never do that if I had a sick child at home. Never."

"I'm sure you wouldn't, because if you had a child you'd just pawn him off on one of your nannies and forget about him. You'd be too busy with your little fundraisers and your designer clothes to worry yourself with actually raising a child."

Alexis shook her head. "You're pathetic. You know, when I first heard you were working for Victor, I thought maybe you'd planned the whole thing at the benefit dinner that night. Maybe he already knew you somehow. Knew you'd get fired. He wanted to paint me as the evil ex-fiancee in front of our friends. But no. I see what happened now. You got fired, fair and square. He felt sorry for you. And now, you're using that precious little boy of yours to win him over." She squared her shoulders. "Because honey, that's all you got. Trust me."

"Are you kidding me? Are you so out of touch with reality that you think a man like Victor Barboza could be won over by a single mom? Do you know how hard it is to date anyone, at all, when you have a child?"

"Well, I can think of no other explanation for why he'd hire someone like you." Alexis shrugged. "Maybe that's what he wanted all along. A child. An insta-family. That's the only thing you have that I don't have. A cute kid he can play with." She let out a loud huff. "I'm sure Victor just loves to go to your house in Newark for a home cooked meal and let your kid play with his car. But it'll get old. You're like a new toy to him. He'll move on soon enough."

"Wait. How'd you know about any of that?"

With a smug grin plastered across her face, Alexis said, "It's a small world. For all you know, maybe Victor told me himself. Maybe he came running to my house after he left yours that night."

In her anger, a million thoughts raced through Cara's mind. But there was one question on her mind. If she had the answer, maybe all of this would start to make sense. "Why did you and Victor break up?"

Alexis chuckled to herself as she walked around to the door of her car and opened it, staring at Cara over the roof. "He cheated on me." Alexis then put her sunglasses back on and slipped inside her car. Her tires squealed when she pounded the gas pedal.

Dumbfounded, Cara stared at Alexis's car until its taillights disappeared.

CHAPTER THIRTEEN

Cara drove home in a zombie-like state. Her altercation with Alexis felt like the world's biggest slap in the face after the euphoria she had experienced when she was out of town with Victor.

She tried to call Victor several times on her way home, but every time, his voicemail picked up. This was not unusual for him. She had heard Gary mention that Victor turned off his phone when he was with a client, to give them his undivided attention. Cara thought best not to leave a voicemail. For one thing, she didn't even know where to start with such a message.

Also, what if she became frantic and sounded as crazy as Alexis?

But what if Alexis wasn't crazy? What if she was completely sane, and she met Cara in that parking lot simply to warn her?

Cara's emotions went from angry to doubtful to everything in between. *How dare that rich witch think she's so much better than me?*

But what if she's right? What if I'm fooling myself to think

Victor could be happy with someone like me for very long? Maybe it's good that Alexis came along to try to burst my bubble.

Still in a daze, Cara finally arrived at home. She parked in the driveway and retrieved her lone suitcase from the trunk to roll it into the house.

As soon as she opened the front door, she heard Isaac's sweet voice.

"Mommy Mommy Mommy!"

She let go of her suitcase and let her purse drop to the floor to scoop him into her arms the moment he ran to her. "My baby boy." She sniffled against unexpected tears. No matter what happened, no matter what kind of crazy emotional roller coaster she may go through because of a man in her life, she could always come home to Isaac. She cradled the back of his head, holding him against her chest. "I love you so much."

Oblivious to her tears, Isaac immediately began talking in a long string of words, some of which were barely audible. When she placed him down on the floor, he kept going, talking with his hands as if he were acting out the events of the past day that she had missed. There were explosions and other sound effects, all of them making Cara laugh as she cried.

After a few minutes, Cara took Isaac's hand and they went to the kitchen where Patty was preparing dinner.

Patty dropped her potholders on the kitchen counter and gave her daughter a hug. "Hello there."

"Hi Mom." Cara squeezed her tight, dreading the inevitable questions. "I hope Isaac wasn't too much trouble without me here."

Patty let her go and gave her a dismissive wave before picking up her potholders. "He's never any trouble. He's my grandson."

"Well you're in an awfully good mood." Cara looked around the kitchen. The last time she saw some of these ingredients was the night her mom had invited Victor for dinner. "Hmm. We're having this dinner again, already?"

"Yes, but this time I made carrot cake."

"What's the occasion? Don't tell me you invited my boss again." Cara sighed.

"What?" Patty stopped what she was doing, giving Cara a wide-eyed stare. "Oh no. You don't wanna see him after your big trip? That's not good. You can tell me all about it later… after," she glanced down at Isaac, who hovered at Cara's feet, "someone goes to bed."

"No, no. It's not that. It's a long story. So tell me. Who's coming over for dinner?"

Isaac spoke up. "Tom. Fwom the pawk."

Patty blushed, devoting her attention to stirring a pot on the stove. "Little one, you are too smart for your own good sometimes."

Cara laughed. "Tom, huh? What happened to Stanley?"

"Oh, nothing." Patty rolled her eyes. "Stanley was so…three weeks ago."

"Wow." Cara's eyes and mouth gaped. "I'm shocked. I don't even know what to say. So, tell me about this Tom. When did you meet him? Is he nice?"

"We met yesterday. He's a widower. Retired from the police force. Has some grandchildren." She giggled. "Likes my cooking."

"How many times do I have to tell you. Everyone likes your cooking."

"Yes, well, it makes me feel good to cook for a man. Call me old-fashioned. Hey, why don't you go get unpacked so you can help me with some things. I'm running a little behind."

"Sure. Is it okay that I invited Marcy over tonight? Didn't know we were having company."

"That's fine. I didn't want her here with your boss because I wanted you to have the spotlight. Tonight's different."

Cara nodded. "Ah. He only has eyes for you."

"I think so, yes."

Cara smiled and led Isaac out of the kitchen.

Fifteen minutes later, as dinner was almost ready, the doorbell rang.

Patty untied her apron and slung it onto the kitchen counter. "I'll get it." She fluffed her hair as she ran to the front door.

Cara gave Patty a minute to greet Tom by herself, then walked out to meet him.

"Hello." Cara held out her hand. "I'm Cara, Patty's daughter."

Tom cleared his throat, his eyes averting hers as if he was nervous. "Pleased to meet you. I'm Tom Sutton."

Cara gave him a big smile in an effort to make him feel more comfortable. *Maybe he's just nervous about meeting the daughter of a love interest. Holy cow, my mom, a love interest?* "So, you and Mom met at the park? Were you there with any of the kids?"

"Um…no," he said. "I was just passing through the area. Went to a deli around the corner."

Right then, the doorbell rang again. Cara stepped around Tom as Patty began to talk to him, leading him into the kitchen.

When Cara opened the front door, she fell forward to give Marcy a quick hug. "Thanks for coming by. You have no idea what a weird day I've had."

"What? Did something happen? Last time we spoke you were doing great."

"I know. I thought about calling you but it was too much to

talk about over the phone. Victor's ex ambushed me in the parking garage."

Marcy's hand went to her chest. She gasped. "No! That's crazy!"

"Yeah."

"What'd she say? What'd she do?"

"Hold on, let's get you inside." Cara stepped back and opened the door wide. "We can go up to my room for some privacy for a minute. Mom has company…" As Marcy walked past her, a car parked on the street caught Cara's eye. It looked like the same blue sedan with dark tinted windows she saw in the parking garage on Monday morning. "Oh my God. What the…"

"What?" Marcy looked over her shoulder at the street. "You see something?"

"Yeah. I swear, Monday morning I had this feeling like someone was watching me before work. It's the same car, I think. I remember the windows. They're so dark, I'm surprised they're legal."

"You think someone's in there watching you right now?" Marcy's voice got quiet. "Like, Mr. Sexy Boss Man? Is he having you followed?"

"I have no idea. I sure hope not." She took one last look at the car, then shut the front door, her heart racing with fear. She walked to the kitchen to find Patty. "Mom, do you know anything about the blue car parked along the street? Has it been there all day?"

"What blue car?" Patty asked.

"It's a blue four door car," Cara said. "Really dark tinted windows."

Tom's eyebrows shot up. "Why do you ask?"

"Oh no." Cara's blood ran cold. "It's yours?" She walked backward as she contemplated taking Isaac's hand and running out the front door. "Were you watching me in the parking garage at work on Monday morning?"

Tom winced, scratching the back of his neck. "I can explain."

Patty's eyes widened. "Monday morning? We didn't meet until yesterday afternoon."

"Please, please, I beg you," Tom said. "Let me explain. I'm sorry if I scared you."

Patty picked up a large kitchen knife from the block behind her. "Stay away from me. I may not look like much but I know how to use this."

Cara glanced around for Isaac. She was relieved to hear him playing loudly in the living room where he couldn't see his grandma threatening a man with a knife.

Tom held up his hands, waving them rapidly in front of him. "Patty, it's really not what you think."

"You better talk fast, mister," Patty said. "Or I'm calling for help."

Tom turned to Cara. "I was hired by Alexis Whitt to spy on you. I'm a private investigator." He looked at Patty. "That's why I was at the park. Alexis wanted me to get information about Isaac, and I already knew where to find you."

Cara was suddenly choked up. "Information about Isaac? What kind of information?"

Tom sighed. "About his paternity. She's desperate to keep you away from Victor. Listen, I'm so sorry." He turned to Patty. "After I left this morning I met with Alexis and told her I can't work for her. I already refunded her retainer. As soon as I met you yesterday, I felt horrible about taking this job. But if I hadn't taken it, I never would've met you. You're the most wonderful, most interesting woman I've met since Dianne died. So for that, I'm grateful to Alexis for hiring me. But that's over. It's really over. I'm so sorry."

Marcy said, "Aw." Her lips curled downward in a sympathetic pout.

Cara shot Marcy a mean look, then directed her attention at Tom. "Why should I believe anything you say? How do we know you're not still spying on me?" She then turned to Patty. "And you! You let a," she lowered her voice in case Isaac could hear, "strange man sleep over, with my son in the house?"

"Sweetie…" Patty said.

"Don't 'sweetie' me," Cara said. "We all just heard him say he left here this morning. You had a stranger in here, overnight. Not only that, but he was the same man who was hired to spy on me."

Patty frowned. "I'm sorry, Cara. We got a little carried away last night, that's all."

Marcy quietly muttered, "Yeah, sounds like it."

Cara gritted her teeth. "I can't believe you two. What does Alexis know about me?"

Tom's head shook. "Not much. I had pictures of your son playing in Victor's car the other night."

Cara gasped. "You took pictures of my son?"

"I'm so sorry," Tom said. "I was doing a job, that's all. I've destroyed those and everything else associated with the case."

"Please calm down, sweetie." Patty walked over to Cara, gently tugging at her elbow. "Come on, let's go talk about this alone."

Cara pulled away from her. "No. You don't understand. I was approached by Alexis Whitt in the parking lot after work tonight. And now I know she wants me away from Victor badly enough to hire someone to spy on my family. This is all too much for me right now. I think I just need to take Isaac and go somewhere by ourselves for dinner. Marcy, you can come, too. But this situation," Cara waved a hand in Tom's general direction, "is something I can't deal with right now."

Several minutes later, Cara was driving with Marcy in the passenger seat and Isaac in the back in his car seat.

"I'm sorry, Marcy," she said. "I can't believe what happened back there."

"It's okay. I'm a little jealous about how exciting your life is compared to mine."

"Ha! I wish mine would calm down. This kind of excitement is a bit much for me right now." Cara shook her head. "Did I tell you I got an offer to go back to my old job in Chicago last week?"

"You're kidding. Why didn't you tell me?"

Cara shrugged. "I don't know. I sorta put it outta my mind, I guess. Didn't want the temptation to take the job. I'm starting to wonder if I made the wrong decision."

"No! You just moved back. Don't leave me all alone here. Besides, what about Victor?"

Isaac giggled. "Bictow!"

Cara looked at him in the rearview mirror. "Yes, Bictow." She gave Marcy a glance and whispered, "Careful what you say in front of him." She let out a loud sigh. "I don't know. Seems like it might be better to get out before it *really* gets serious. This whole Alexis thing." Cara gripped her steering wheel like she wanted to shake it out of place. "You know, she told me today that…" She glanced at Isaac again and lowered her voice. "Let's just say, she claimed there was infidelity on his part."

"Well, she sounds insane," Marcy said. "I wouldn't put it past her to lie. If she went as far as hiring a private investigator—"

Cara produced a deep groan. "Don't remind me. Mom. I can't believe it."

"Cara hon, I know you don't wanna hear this but…" Marcy paused, considering how to soften what she wanted to say. "I think you may be overreacting about your mom and Tom. He seemed pretty sincere. He could've just taken the money and finished the job but he didn't. He quit."

"So he says…"

"Whatever. I'm sure he could prove it. Listen, how many times has your mom dated since your dad passed? Hmm?"

"I don't know."

"Well, I always kept in touch with her, even when you didn't live here. Trust me, she doesn't date." Marcy smiled. "I think it's sweet."

Cara's voice was weak. "Yeah, maybe. But did she have to let him…" She glanced at Isaac and quietly said, "spend the night."

"Like mother like daughter," Marcy said.

Cara's mouth fell open. She took her hand off the steering wheel and smacked Marcy's leg. "How dare you throw that up in my face! It's been years for me."

"I repeat. Like mother, like daughter." Marcy burst into hysterics.

Cara gave Isaac another look, thankful he had distracted himself by staring out the window. Hopefully he wouldn't be repeating, "Like mother, like daughter," for the rest of the night.

* * *

"Hold my calls," Victor said to Gary, then shut his office door to speak to Cara privately. During their brief phone call the night before, she seemed distant. This morning, he cleared his schedule to meet with her to hopefully find out why her mood toward him had changed so much.

The answer was simple: Alexis.

Cara was obviously shaken up, and he couldn't blame her. The person he blamed was himself, for not seeing Alexis for who she truly was all along.

He took a seat beside Cara and rolled his chair forward until he was close enough to place his hand on hers. "I'm deeply sorry for what happened yesterday. I had no idea she would invade your privacy like that. Would it help if I had someone escort you through the parking garage from now on?"

She pulled her hand away from his. "No. It's more than that. She had a man taking pictures of you with my son. Do you know how creepy that makes me feel?"

"Cara, sweetheart, I'm so sorry—"

"How do I know what else she's capable of? She's rich and probably crazy and I have a child to protect—"

"Cara!" He leaned forward in his chair, his eyes fixed on hers. "I'll handle Alexis. I'll make sure she never bothers you again."

She folded her hands in her lap as she stared at the wall, dazed. "Did you cheat on her?"

"What? Why in the world would you think that?"

"That's what she told me yesterday."

"Oh my God." Instantly, Victor seethed with rage. He cracked one knuckle and took a deep breath before answering. "No. I absolutely did *not* cheat on her."

"Then, what happened? Why'd you break up?" Cara's eyebrows furrowed. "You know, I don't think I'll ever understand why you were with someone like her in the first place. Did you not realize what an evil brat she was?"

He grabbed the arm of Cara's chair and spun her around, forcing her to face him. "I asked myself that same question for a long time after we broke up. How did I not see how immature and selfish she was? How did I not know she was screwing Esteban, her personal trainer, behind my back?"

Cara winced. "Oh…"

"Yeah." He nodded. "She's the one who cheated. And you're

the first person I've ever told about it, so I'm going to trust you not to repeat it."

"What do you mean? Why haven't you told anyone? She could be lying to others about you."

"I have too much respect for her family to drag their name through the mud because of her indiscretion. Her father is a valuable mentor of mine. The honorable thing to do was simply break off the engagement and forget about her. Move on like I never knew her." He sighed. "But she won't let me forget."

"How long were you engaged?"

"Longer than I care to admit." Victor held up his hand to halt her response. "I know what you're gonna say. How did I let her make such a fool out of me? The answer is, I was too busy building my career to get to know her like I should have. I won't make that mistake again. She was obviously someone I didn't know at all. But I learned my lesson. I know what's really important now. I see so many things in you that she'll never have."

"You do?"

"Yes. You're hardworking. Humble. Nurturing." His palm grazed her cheek, his voice gentle. "And you're beautiful. Please, let me get to know you, Cara. Don't let her scare you away from me."

Entranced by his sweetness, Cara could only gaze into his eyes, unable to form a response.

Victor rose from his chair, bending forward to pull her into a kiss.

Nothing in Cara wanted to resist him. The last of her worries disappeared, drawn away by the heat of his lips and replaced by memories of yesterday, of how incredible it felt to let him take her. The memories rushed back, along with her desire to be taken again.

He kissed her until he found himself dying to part her

thighs. He forced himself to pull away. "I'm sorry, *querida*," he whispered. "I need to stop or I'll spend the next hour pleasuring you and there's a meeting I must attend."

"Oh, Cara." He kissed her ear. "I'm never gonna get any work done with you around."

"Sorry."

"Don't be sorry. I was working too much anyway." He smiled and gave her a soft peck on the lips. "But I do have a meeting. I'll see you soon. Lunch, okay?"

"Yes. I can't wait."

Cara left Victor's office, blushing when Gary gave her a wink out in the hall.

CHAPTER FOURTEEN

"Well, it's taken long enough. You better have some amazing news for me." Alexis paced the grand hallway in her parents' house, holding her phone to her ear. Four days had passed since she approached Cara Green in the parking garage at Monarch Enterprises. Her new private investigator, Lindy, came highly recommended. But so far, Alexis was disappointed. There were more pictures of Victor playing with Cara's sickeningly-cute kid, and little else. Alexis had to be more careful now. Victor's attorney had filed a restraining order against Alexis on behalf of Cara. It included a section about the use of investigators. If there was proof that Alexis, or anyone hired by Alexis, came within seventy-five yards of the Green family, they would be in violation of the order.

Alexis lost no sleep over the fact that her former flame had taken legal action against her. She was certain Victor would eventually come to his senses and they could pick up where they left off, leaving all of this ugliness behind them.

Lindy said, "*Remember that connection I told you about at the hospital?"*

"Yes."

"She finally got back to me. I have a full copy of little Isaac Green's file."

"Okay." Alexis stopped pacing, her heart beating with anticipation. "And there's something helpful in it?" She had wished all along they could find the boy's father and possibly give Cara a reason to break up with Victor.

"I believe so. All of my research so far has told me Cara never knew who the father was. She says she got pregnant from a one night stand in college and never saw the guy again. There's no father listed on the birth certificate." She paused for a breath. *"However, there's a family medical history form here with some info about the father. It says his blood type is B positive and there was a history of diabetes and cancer in his family."*

"Really? Interesting…"

"Yes. So, unless she's lying on the form, and I doubt she is, it sounds to me like she knows the father. Blood type and family illnesses aren't something most college kids talk about on a one night stand."

"Does it have his name?"

"No, they didn't ask for it."

"And you really think it means something? Maybe she did her own research after she found out she was pregnant."

"It's possible, but from my experience, unless they're hiding something, single women always want that name on the birth certificate. It helps their chances of getting child support. If she knows the father's medical history, I bet she knows who he is. She was struggling financially before Victor hired her. Don't you think she would've wanted some help from her baby's father? To me, this says she's hiding something."

"What do you think she's hiding?"

"Not sure. She's ashamed of the father, maybe? Doesn't want any

connection to him. Could've been a really bad break up. Want me to track him down?"

Alexis gasped. "Do you think you can?"

"I'm already on it."

* * *

Two weeks later, Cara sat next to Victor, cuddling up to him on the park bench next to the playground. They both watched Isaac climb to the top of a slide where he stood up and yelled, "Bictow! Watch me, Bictow!"

"I'm watching!" Victor yelled back at him.

Isaac quickly slid down to the bottom. When his feet hit the ground, Cara and Victor applauded and cheered, making Isaac smile before he ran off to a swing set where a friend from the neighborhood waited to give him a push.

"I wish I had that much energy." Victor chuckled. His arm was draped around her shoulders, his hand rubbing her arm. "So, Patty's meeting Tom's family today?"

She chuckled with a hint of sarcasm. "Yes. It's their big two week anniversary. He surprised her this morning by asking her to an early dinner. That's why I lost my babysitter for the afternoon."

"So, she's spending the night at his place?"

"Yes."

He nodded and kissed the top of her head. "I hope that means I can spend the night at *your* place, then."

"I suppose." She giggled. "You know, when I asked for the afternoon off, I had no idea you would leave the office and come to the playground with me."

Victor sighed. "I know. I have to stop putting work before everything else. Besides, I hadn't seen Isaac in a few days. I don't want him to forget who I am."

"I wouldn't worry about that. He talks about you all the time."

"Really?" He smiled. "That's good." He paused, gentling his voice. "Does that still make you nervous?"

Cara took a hesitant breath. "Not as much. But yes."

He nodded. "I understand. I know it must be hard. My mother was the same way. She always said me and my brothers were the reason she didn't date. Didn't want us getting attached." He grinned as he watched Isaac playing on the swing. "So…uh…you ever think about having more?"

"More?"

"Yes." Victor cleared his throat and added, "More children."

Cara was startled by his question. Occasionally, Victor sneaked a question into their casual conversations that indicated he already saw a future with her, even though they had only known each other a matter of weeks. This was definitely one of those questions, and once again, she was caught off guard. "Um…maybe. I hadn't really thought about it."

"If you met the right person, perhaps?" His arm tightened, pulling her a bit closer.

Her heart pounded a fierce beat. She looked at Victor's face, but his eyes were fixed on Isaac. For the first time, she felt her fear slowly begin to slip away in response to his sincerity. She momentarily thought of exploring the idea and asking how many children he wanted, and how soon. Instead, her logic took over, and she decided against it. That was a conversation for later. *Much* later. For now, she closed her eyes and relaxed against Victor's chest with the knowledge that if she wasn't watching Isaac on the playground, Victor was.

An hour later they walked the three blocks back to Cara's house. Isaac babbled excitedly with Victor, continuing as they walked through the front door.

Cara bent down to pick up the letters that had been shoved inside their mail slot while they were gone.

Along with a utility bill and some junk mail was a greeting card for Cara. It came in a bright yellow envelope with no return address, no stamp, no postmark.

Since her birthday was three months away, Cara opened it with a strange curiosity as she listened to Isaac tell Victor about his favorite fast food restaurant, where he was absolutely dying to eat tonight.

The card was pretty on the outside, with bright yellow roses and the word, "Greetings."

But the message written inside made Cara's skin crawl.

"I know what you're hiding about his father. Will you tell V before I do?"

That witch! Cara knew this had to be the work of Alexis, who had most likely been waiting for just the right time to drop off a message like this. The restraining order had been in effect for two weeks now, and Cara thought Alexis had given up. She took a deep breath to calm down. Not only had Alexis not given up, but she seemed to be back with ammunition.

Briefly, Cara wanted to get Victor's attention and show him the message. Get Alexis in trouble. Even though she didn't sign it, any reasonable person would know who wrote it.

But right then, she saw Victor get on his knees on the living room floor. He was engrossed in Isaac's story of how he obtained his latest toy—a large red plastic race car—by behaving good all of Saturday afternoon. Cara almost teared up. Isaac was the kind of toddler who made friends everywhere he went, and yet he had never taken to anyone as quickly as he had taken to Victor. Maybe it was good for Isaac to have a good male role model in his life. Would Victor someday be Isaac's stepfather? She had no clue. And, in spite of her fear and logic, she had started to like the idea.

Cara slipped the greeting card into her purse, unnoticed. Tonight was not the night for a conversation about the man who had gotten her pregnant. Isaac was certainly too young to understand. And if Victor heard Cara's side, she assumed he would see why she kept Isaac a secret from his father.

Or would he? Cara's stomach twisted as she thought about it.

Alexis had gone too far this time, and Cara refused to be bullied. She took a seat on the couch, thinking about her own form of retaliation. *How dare she stalk me and threaten me over my own son?*

* * *

The next morning, Cara and Victor shared their usual "see you later" kiss in his office before he went off to attend the first of many meetings.

As soon as she saw him turn the corner to take the elevator, she walked up to Gary's desk.

"Yes?" Gary smiled.

"Do you have a number on file for Alexis Whitt? Cell phone, preferably."

His lips formed a scowl. He pushed his mouthpiece away and leaned forward. "Why?"

"I just need to speak with her. It's important."

"Does Mr. Barboza know about this?"

"No. Does he have to?"

He lifted one brow. "Yes."

Cara let out a groan. "Why?"

"He made it very clear after the incident a few weeks ago that she was not welcome here under any circumstances. That includes phone calls."

"Well, yeah. She's not supposed to call here. But did he say anything about one of us calling her?"

His eyes rolled. "He didn't really have to, did he? He will certainly want to know if you contact her and I won't feel comfortable keeping it a secret."

"Come on, Gary. Please. I just need to talk to her this one time. That's all. It's really important. I have to get a few things off my chest."

Gary's eyebrows momentarily shot up at the thought of what Cara might say to her. "I suppose it wouldn't hurt if you promise to tell Mr. Barboza about it as soon as possible."

Cara nodded. "I will."

"Okay. If you don't, I'll tell him myself when he comes back to his office. Got it?"

With a cynical chuckle, she said, "Does he have any idea how loyal you are?"

"Actually, I think he does." His eyes narrowed at her. "And I can't afford to damage my reputation." He turned to his computer and clicked a few times, then scrawled a number on a memo pad and handed it to Cara. "Here. Use it wisely. And by that I mean, put her in her place."

Cara smiled and said, "I will," over her shoulder as she rushed to her office. She immediately shut the door behind her.

* * *

Alexis hummed a tune to herself as she waved goodbye to some friends at the country club. She was fresh out of the shower after an early morning tennis match.

As she trotted through the parking lot, her phone vibrated in her purse.

"Holy crap!" Alexis let out a tiny squeal when she saw the name "Chubby Green" on her caller ID. She programmed this mean nickname for Cara in her phone weeks earlier with no intention of actually calling her. Seeing it today made her giddy. *I finally got under her skin.*

Alexis stood still, smiling ear to ear, and answered the phone in her cheeriest voice. "Alexis Whitt speaking."

Cara's tone was cold. *"You can do whatever you want to me but leave my son out of it."*

Alexis waited a few moments then let out a long sigh. "I don't know what you're talking about."

"Oh, please. You're lucky I haven't reported you for violating the restraining order. I know you were spying on us yesterday. I'm trying to be nice to you."

She produced a single laugh. "That's unlikely. You have something to hide and you know it. That's why you called me yourself instead of getting Victor involved."

"No. I'm trying to have mercy on you. Take the high road. I feel very sorry for you."

"There's no reason anyone should feel sorry for me. Especially you. I know you're hiding your son's paternity because you don't know how Victor will react. He never knew his own father."

"Exactly what do you think I'm hiding?"

"If you have nothing to hide, then why are you asking?"

"Because it involves my son. What is it you think you know about me?"

Alexis had no hard evidence, and her private investigator, Lindy, had found this a difficult task. She chose to bluff, using Lindy's reasoning. "You tell everyone his father was a fling and you never knew him, but you did. You knew him very well. And you chose not to tell the man about his own son."

Cara was silent.

Alexis continued. "Victor told me *so* many times he wished he could remember more about his father. How do you think he would react to the news that he's involved with a woman who is cruel enough to withhold that kind of love from her own flesh and blood?"

Alexis heard silence, then what sounded like muffled sniffling. *Is she crying? This went way better than I could've hoped for.*

When Cara finally spoke again, her voice was shaky. "*You're a terrible person. No matter what happens to me and Victor, he's never gonna want you back.*" And then she hung up.

"Woo-hoo!" Alexis shouted as she dropped her phone in her purse and dug out her keys. *I have her right where I want her.* Hopefully Lindy would be able to dig up some reliable information on the father, soon. Whatever it took to get Cara Green's big, fat claws out of Victor…

She hopped into her car and checked her reflection in the rearview mirror, applying a fresh layer of lipstick. She was just about to put her car in reverse when her purse vibrated.

She giggled. *I hope it's her again.*

Her giggling stopped when she saw her mother's name and picture.

"Good morning, Mother."

Alexis was greeted by loud sobs.

"Mother?" She turned off the ignition. "Mother! What's wrong?"

"*Darling…your father…*"

"What?" Alexis was instantly frantic. Her mother was not the type of woman who cried easily. This meant there was something desperately wrong. "What happened to Daddy? Mother!"

"*Come to the hospital. Now.*"

CHAPTER FIFTEEN

Victor arrived on the sixth floor of the hospital to find Colleen Whitt crying as she paced the hall outside her husband's room. A few people he knew in passing sat in plastic chairs against the wall. They each gave Victor a solemn look.

"Victor!" Colleen reached out for him. "Thank you. I'm sorry I had to bother you."

"It's no bother." He put his arms around her, letting her shake as she sobbed against him. "I'm so sorry," he whispered.

Colleen stayed in his embrace until she could speak without crying. Then she pulled away and said, "It's not good. He had a massive stroke."

"Oh no. I'm so sorry."

"Well…" Her face crumbled in tears, which she quickly wiped away with a tissue before taking a deep breath, steeling herself. Her voice was quiet. "He's asking for you. There's been some memory loss. He thinks you and Alexis are still together. She's in there with him right now."

Victor winced as a thin layer of tears covered his eyes.

Instantly, he was racked with guilt over doing such a poor job of staying in touch with Douglas. "So I should talk to him?"

Colleen nodded. "If you don't mind. He thinks of you as the son he never had." She sniffled. "I'm so sorry for the way it all turned out."

He shook his head and put his arms around her, but she pushed him away.

"No," she said. "Hurry. Please." She motioned toward the closed door behind her.

Victor was about to open it when a nurse bustled through from inside as she scribbled notes on a chart and hurried down the hall. Alexis stood at the side of the bed with genuine tears flowing across her cheeks. Victor had never seen her so frightened, and his heart filled with sympathy for her. He rushed to her side, placing a gentle hand on her back as he saw Douglas lying in bed. There were tubes all over him. Machines all around the room beeped and made noises. And Douglas looked small and shriveled; a shadow of the husky, jolly man everyone knew him to be.

Alexis held his hand as her fingers stroked his gray hair. "It'll be okay, Daddy. It'll be okay."

Douglas could barely open his mouth to speak. "Daughter... sweet daughter...sweet girl." His eyes, barely focusing, drifted to Victor. "Son. Come here...son."

Alexis stepped back to give Victor space, gesturing at him to take her place beside her father.

Victor moved forward and took Douglas's hand. "I'm here."

"Good." Douglas spoke just above a whisper. "Victor...take good care...of my girl..."

Victor's eyes filled with tears at the thought of losing his dear friend. He didn't dare correct him. Instead, he squeezed his hand tightly and said, "I will, sir."

Douglas inhaled deeply, wheezing until he had enough air

to speak. "A legacy…children…many children…"

Victor took several tissues from the box at the side of the bed and pressed them against his closed eyes. They had this conversation many times while he was still engaged to Alexis. Douglas confided in Victor that one of his biggest regrets was not having more children; Alexis was an only child. But Douglas seemed satisfied that Victor and Alexis could go on to have a large family. Douglas always called it a legacy. But now, there was no hope of that. At least, not for Victor and Alexis. Douglas's memory loss made this tragic situation much sadder for Victor, who forced a grin and said, "We will, sir."

Victor was startled by the door opening and two doctors rushing into the room.

"Excuse me," one of the doctors said as he pushed past Victor, who saw Alexis leaving and followed her.

Colleen was on her phone, talking and crying. Alexis walked to a row of empty chairs.

Victor sat beside her, his hand on her knee. "I'm so sorry about your father."

Alexis shook her head and pushed his hand away. "Don't." She reached for tissues from a box that sat in the unoccupied chair beside her.

"I'm sorry. Didn't mean to—"

"Quit saying you're sorry, Victor." She blotted her eyes. "That's all I've heard for the past hour. Everyone's sorry. The nurses are sorry. Mother's sorry. You're sorry. *Sorry* won't change anything." Her mouth formed a deep frown. She gasped for air. "He's not gonna make it. Doesn't matter how sorry anyone is."

"Don't say that. This is a great hospital. He's getting the best care. Besides, he was healthy until this. He—"

"No, he wasn't." She shook her head as tears fell to her cheeks. "He's not healthy at all. His doctors have warned him for years to take better care of himself."

Victor searched for the right words to say until he realized there probably weren't any. This situation was nothing he could fix. All he could do was hope and pray that his friend would get better, and come out of it stronger and healthier than ever. He was about to go look for the hospital chapel when Alexis spoke up.

"I did this," Alexis said in a grave tone.

Stunned, Victor asked, "What are you talking about?"

"I did this. I'm the reason he's in there."

"How?"

"Karma." Alexis sniffled as she wiped her cheeks. "Fate. God."

Victor had never heard her speak of such things. Alexis's topics of discussion were usually more superficial. It was as if she had aged thirty years in a matter of minutes. "No. It doesn't work that way," he said. He thought about the havoc she had wreaked in his life lately. From the moment he walked onto this floor and saw Colleen, he had pushed it all to the back of his mind. But it all came roaring to the forefront now. And still, he knew no matter what Alexis did, what heinous acts she committed, she was not to blame for her father's crisis. "You didn't do this, Alexis."

"How else do you explain it then?" She stared straight ahead. "I don't believe in coincidence. I never have. Daddy taught me that. We make our own way in this world." She turned to Victor. "Please tell Cara I'm sorry. I'll never bother either of you again." She stood and walked numbly down the hall.

* * *

It was almost time to leave work after a boring day at the office. Cara looked at the clock for the hundredth time. She hadn't seen Victor since early this morning. Her only communication with him was a short, cryptic email sent from his phone that said he was at the hospital with a sick friend and would explain later.

After her conversation with Alexis, Cara had been too nervous to eat or focus on work. *What if she was right? What if Victor doesn't understand?*

She planned to tell him the entire story about Isaac's father over dinner tonight. Victor made reservations for two at a cozy Italian restaurant a few blocks from the office. As the hour drew closer, she worried he had forgotten. *Just as well*, she thought. *I'm in no mood to eat.*

Gary poked his head into her office and said, "Have a good night, Cara," just as she heard her phone ring.

"You too!" Her heart thumped with excitement, hoping to soon hear that Victor was on his way. But when she saw the name of her former manager in Chicago, she groaned her disappointment and clicked the button to ignore the call, assuming she would soon hear from Victor.

Seconds later, Justine called again.

Cara grimaced at the phone as if it were a real person. "Not now!" As she listened to it ring a few more times, she rolled her eyes and decided to answer, only to have a distraction from her worries about Victor. "Hi Justine. How ya doin'?"

"I'm fine but I'd be doing much better if I could get one of my most talented employees back. How are you?"

Not this again. Cara ignored the two emails Justine had sent her since their talk a few weeks earlier. "I'm all right. My new job keeps me very busy."

"I'm sure it does. But Cara, I really need you. I wish I'd never had to let you go in the first place but it wasn't my decision to make."

"I know, but I'm sure you'll find someone soon. There are so many people looking for jobs right now and—"

"*Yes, but not many with your experience. I need someone who can hit the ground running, and I need them now. I've interviewed fifteen people and in the back of my mind I keep thinking, if only I could get another Cara…*"

"I'm sorry. I feel your pain but I just can't. My new boss needs me, too."

"*No, he can't need you as badly as I do.*"

Cara laughed. She hadn't told Justine about her romantic involvement with Victor. "I'm not so sure about that."

"*Come on. I wasn't that horrible to work for, was I?*"

"No, it has nothing to do with that. You know I loved working with you. I was just telling someone the other day about how we used to go out for drinks after work sometimes."

"*I miss that. We had a really good group.*" Justine sighed. "*Come on. Tell me what I have to do.*"

"There's nothing you can—"

"*How's a ten grand sign-on bonus sound? In addition to relocation expenses?*"

"No, I really can't—"

"*Twenty grand. That's as high as I can go. And you'll start out at fifteen grand over what you were making when you left.*"

"I can't be worth that much."

"*Yes, you can. Compared to the cost of hiring someone new who doesn't have your experience? You're a steal.*"

Cara whined as she spoke. "I'm sorry. It hurts me to say no but I have to. If only you'd called me before I got this job…"

"*Yeah, yeah.*" Justine's tone was sad. "*Well, call me if you change your mind in the next few days. I'll have to make a decision to hire someone else soon.*"

"I will." Cara's phone beeped. "I'm sorry, I gotta go. Getting another call."

"*Okay, bye.*"

"Bye." Cara took a deep breath when she saw it was Victor. "Hello?"

"*Hello, querida.*" He yawned. "*I'm sorry. How rude of me. It's been an exhausting day.*"

"What happened? Who's in the hospital?"

He paused for a long moment. "*Douglas Whitt.*"

Cara gulped. "You mean, Alexis's dad?"

"*Yes.*"

She shook her head, confused. "Why are you there? Did she call you? Why would you spend all day at the hospital with her?"

"*It wasn't about her. He was my friend.*" Victor's voice was quiet and sober. "*And he didn't make it. He passed away a little over an hour ago. Massive stroke.*"

"Oh no. I'm so sorry."

"*Me too. He was a great man. I'll miss him.*"

Cara held the phone to her ear with no idea what to say. All day, Alexis had been in her head, tormenting her with anger and doubt. And now, that woman's own father was dead? It was hard to imagine.

After a while, Victor inhaled deeply, then said, "*I'll have to cancel our dinner plans tonight. And since I had to shift my schedule around today, I may not see much of you tomorrow. I'm sorry.*"

"I understand."

"*Good.*" He sighed in relief. "*Before I go, I need to tell you Alexis apologized for everything. Says she feels terrible about it.*"

Cara scoffed. "Yeah, okay. I don't know what to say to that."

"*Me neither. It really surprised me.*"

"You don't really think she's changed, do you?"

"*I think she's in shock. She's grieving. Probably saying a lot of things.*"

Startled by the genuine sympathy she sensed in his tone, she let a few thoughts slip loose, in haste. "Is that why you've been with her all day? Are you comforting her? Will you be with her tonight?"

"*No! God, Cara. I'm here because Douglas was asking for me. And yes, I've tried to be kind to Alexis. Her father just died. I'm not heartless.*"

"I didn't mean to imply you were. I'm just a little confused."

Victor yawned again. "*It's fine. We'll talk about it later, okay? I've gotta go. I'm sorry.*"

Several minutes later, Cara was alone with her thoughts as she drove home. Her mind was still reeling from the news about Alexis's father. Having lost her own father as a teenager, Cara wanted to have some empathy for Alexis but all she could think about was the cruelty Alexis had shown her. Surely, she was crazy enough to use even this tragic situation for her own gain. She could see it in her mind. Alexis batting her eyelashes at Victor, playing on his kindness.

Victor wouldn't fall for that, would he?

When Cara entered her mother's house for the night, Isaac jumped up into her arms as usual. She hugged him extra tight.

Patty strolled in from the kitchen as Cara was setting Isaac on the floor. "What are you doing home so early? You should've called while you were on the way. I figured you'd call later to tell me you were staying the night with you-know-who."

"You know who" had become their code name for Victor when Isaac was around because every time the toddler heard the name "Victor" he nearly threw a fit and demanded to see him.

Cara let out a sad sigh. "It's a long story. He had to cancel because Alexis's father died today."

"Oh no." Patty brought her hand to her chest. "She didn't

have something to do with it, did she? You know, to get an early inheritance?"

"I don't think she's *that* crazy. Supposedly, he had a stroke."

"Hmm." She nodded, deep in thought. "What's that have to do with him canceling dinner?"

"He was close to her dad. Really close." Cara looked around to make sure Isaac was occupied with toys on the living room floor. She then lowered her voice. "It's so strange to me. He told me Alexis apologized. She feels bad about everything."

"About what, exactly?"

"All he said was she feels bad about *everything*." Cara shrugged. "I don't know. I assume for all the spying. Harassment. Getting me fired. He was so brief on the phone. Said he was tired."

"I can tell you're worried." Patty put her hand on Cara's shoulder. "It'll be all right. I'm sure he'll make it up to you soon."

"I don't know. He seemed so distant. He didn't even say when we'd see each other again."

"Don't do that." Patty waggled a finger. "Don't be the needy girlfriend. There's no better way to scare a man off."

"It's not *that*, Mom. I don't need his constant attention." Cara turned around to watch Isaac. "How stupid am I to get involved with my boss? I could lose everything if he doesn't want me anymore. He said I shouldn't be scared. He'd find me another job or whatever. But what if he doesn't? And what about *him*?" She nodded toward Isaac. "He's already so attached."

"I think you're overreacting. You-know-who had a bad day and he canceled dinner. End of story. Don't overthink it."

Cara's eyes were still on Isaac. "Justine called me again today."

"Justine? In Chicago?"

"Yeah. Offered me a lot of money to come back. A *lot* of money."

Patty winced. "Oh boy." She could see in her daughter's eyes that she was seriously considering the offer. Cara was always too practical. Wise beyond her years. Patty's eyes welled up at the thought of Cara and Isaac leaving. "I hope you won't do that."

Cara cleared her throat, choking away tears of her own. "I was careless to let myself get so swept away. It'd be different if it was just me but I have a kid to think about. We need security."

"But sweetie, nothing's secure these days. You could take that job and be laid off again."

"That could happen here, too. You just said it—nothing's secure. And at least with Justine, I don't have to worry about me and my son both getting our hearts broken by my boss." Cara slid her hand across her cheek to get rid of a tear as she turned to her mom. "Maybe her phone call was perfect timing."

Patty stuck her palm to her forehead, her eyes closed. "I have to go finish dinner. Please don't make any rash decisions. At least sleep on the idea."

Cara watched Patty go to the kitchen before sitting on the couch, where she quietly burst into tears. Thankfully, Isaac was too busy crashing toy cars together to notice.

CHAPTER SIXTEEN

Victor placed his hand on Colleen Whitt's shoulder. "Please let me know if you need anything." It was the morning after Douglas's passing, and Victor had dropped by the Whitt estate before beginning the business of the day. He sat alone with her on a plush sofa in the parlor.

"I will." She nodded weakly.

"And again, I'm so sorry I won't be able to attend the memorial service in Kentucky. I've tried to work it out on my calendar—"

"Shh." Her eyes narrowed as she patted his hand. "You've done enough, Victor. Much more than you should've. It means so much to me that you came to the hospital yesterday." With a sad sigh, she added. "It's a shame about you and Alexis. Douglas always spoke of you so highly. It did his heart good to see you." Colleen's tiny grin faded and she brought a tissue to her eyes, taking a deep breath to steady herself. She opened her mouth to speak again when she turned sharply in response to a loud noise from the kitchen. She then rolled her eyes and said, "Caterers. Sounds like they're tearing the house apart just to set up a small brunch."

"You're having a brunch today?"

"Yes. To feed the lawyers coming over. There's so much business to settle."

"You should have someone else do that for you. I can make some calls."

Colleen sniffled and shook her head. "No. I need to stay busy or I'll fall apart." Another sound came from the kitchen as she rose to her feet. "Oh dear." She gave Victor a frantic look.

"I'll show myself out." Victor stood up and gave her one last small hug. She scurried off toward the kitchen as Victor headed in the opposite direction.

He was only a few steps from heading out the front door when he heard a voice calling his name from the grand staircase behind him. He groaned inwardly as he turned around to see Alexis descending the stairs.

When he caught a glimpse of her short lacy form-fitting nightgown, he stared away from her, at the wall. "Good morning, Alexis. I was just paying my condolences to your mother. I have to go."

"Leaving already?" Her bare feet were light as she raced to the bottom and walked up to him. "Weren't you going to say anything to me?"

"I really need to get to the office. And I think you probably need to put some clothes on." Victor glanced around the large entryway, looking for the butler. "Where's Clifford, by the way?" Surely Alexis didn't usually walk around the house in such skimpy clothes where the help could see her. She had to be doing this for him.

"He's probably helping Mother in the kitchen. What? Am I making you uncomfortable?"

Victor cleared his throat and set his eyes on hers, careful to look nowhere else. "I'm deeply sorry for your loss, Alexis."

Tears filled her eyes, her voice cracking as she spoke. "Thank you. It doesn't seem real to me yet." She quickly wiped her tears away with her fingertips. "So, will you be taking the private jet to the memorial service?"

"No. I won't be attending."

"What? Why not?"

"I just can't work it out. I already explained it to—"

Alexis inched closer. "But I need you. Remember? Daddy asked you to take care of me."

"He wasn't in his right mind. You know that. I need to—"

She interrupted by launching her scantily clad body against his, her arms tight around his back. "Please stay." She cried against his suit. "It's been so nice to be with you again. I need you."

Victor stood completely still, arms at his sides. "Let go of me, Alexis."

"Please, Victor!"

He lifted his hands against the front of her shoulders, pushing her away. He stayed there for a moment longer as he looked in her eyes to make sure she heard him. "Don't test me. I'm sympathetic, but nothing's changed. We're over, and you need to leave Cara alone." He let go of her and straightened his tie as he prepared to leave.

"Cara." Alexis let out a disgusted huff.

"You apologized yesterday. Remember?"

"Yes. But that doesn't change how I feel about you. I'll always want you back." She stared at him, pleading. "I know you got involved with her after I got her fired. If you're trying to prove a point, consider it proven. I've learned my lesson. Please, stop punishing me."

"Punishing you?" Victor chuckled as he turned to exit. "Cara is not your punishment. She's my reward." He opened the door.

He had only taken a few steps outside when he heard Alexis behind him.

She said, "You may want to ask *your reward* why she didn't tell her baby's father she was pregnant."

Victor stopped. "Excuse me?" He looked back at her, one eyebrow raised.

She took a flirtatious stance in the open doorway, a hand on her hip. "Yeah. I'll bet she's never mentioned that, has she? I think it's terrible when a mother keeps a young boy from knowing his own father, don't you?"

In his calmest voice, Victor replied, "I'm sure she had her reasons. Now, leave us alone or there *will* be consequences." In no mood to ask how she had obtained such information, he walked to his car without looking back.

* * *

It was almost lunch time, and Cara hadn't heard from Victor all day. No text message, no email. Just silence. And every time she caught herself wondering if he was somewhere comforting Alexis, she distracted herself with thoughts of Chicago. Usually, she restricted her personal Internet searches to her phone, but today she didn't care. The search history from her computer would clearly show a person who was contemplating a serious move.

The clock struck noon and Cara was seconds away from reaching for her purse to go to lunch when Rhonda appeared at her door. With a blank look on her face, Rhonda waved and said, "Hey."

"Hey there. You okay?"

"Yeah. You got a minute?"

"I guess so. Have a seat." Cara motioned to the seat beside her desk.

Rhonda looked outside for Gary, who was nowhere to be seen, then closed the door and sat down. "Do you know Sally in accounting?"

"I don't think so."

"Well, anyway, she sent me something and told me to show it to you. It's in my personal email." Rhonda winced as she handed her phone to Cara. "I'm not sure what it means to you, exactly…"

Confused, Cara took the phone. "A video?" Then she immediately hit play. It was a short clip with no sound. She saw a woman, who looked like Alexis from behind, speaking to Victor. "What the…she's almost naked."

"I know."

"Is this a security video?" Cara gasped when she saw Alexis fall against Victor's chest. The video ended a few seconds later. "Were they kissing? I can't tell from this weird angle."

Rhonda shrugged. "I don't know. I'm really sorry. I don't know why she wanted you to see that."

Cara gaped at the video as she hit play for a second time. "This date stamp says today. Oh my God…"

"Oh sweetie." Rhonda frowned. "The rumors are true, aren't they? You and Barboza?"

Cara put her elbows on her desk, her palms against her forehead. "Oh my God…oh my God…"

"Oh no. I'm sorry. I hear he's a heartbreaker. If I were you I'd—"

"Get out." Cara put her hands down on her desk, glaring at Rhonda.

"Please, let me help—"

"No. Get out. And close the door behind you."

Without another word, Rhonda stood and walked out the door. As soon as it closed, Cara clicked her mouse to open a new browser window. "I'm *so* done with this."

* * *

Patty answered the door just as Victor was about to ring the doorbell for the second time. She heaved forward, sighing in relief as she greeted him. "Well, aren't you a sight for sore eyes."

Victor walked inside as she closed the door behind him. "Is Cara here? I've been trying to call her all afternoon. My assistant said she left early and…" He stopped talking when he realized Patty was crying. "Oh no. What happened?"

He was startled when Isaac ran into the room screaming, "Mommy Mommy Mommy!" as he usually did that time of the day to welcome his mom home for the evening. Isaac stopped at Victor's feet, his eyes lighting up as he inhaled a slow gasp, excited to see his friend. He reached up and put his hand around Victor's thumb, ready to pull him into the living room. "Wook what I got—"

Patty tapped Isaac's shoulder. "No, sweetie. Not now."

Isaac's face instantly puckered. He produced a high-pitched whine.

Victor bent down to hoist him up into his arms. "Hey buddy." He patted his back. "*Mi amigo.*"

Isaac smiled at that. He let his head fall against Victor's chest for a moment, then leaned back to look in his eyes as he began a story. "Today me and Gwammah…"

Victor nodded along and tried to interpret as much of Isaac's chatter as he could, asking occasional questions for clarification. He slowly walked to the living room and sat down, keeping Isaac on his knee. Patty sat beside them. When Isaac finished talking, he hopped out of Victor's lap and walked a few feet away where he sat on the floor and turned his attention to a television show he had forgotten he was watching.

Patty teared up again. "See? You're so good with him." Her voice got softer in case Isaac could hear. "I don't know why my daughter's so stubborn about you."

He placed a gentle hand on her arm. "Please tell me what happened."

"She swore me to secrecy, of course." She chuckled sadly and wiped her eyes. "I'm not supposed to tell you she's on her way to Chicago. Going back to her old job."

"What?" Victor's heart raced with worry. "Without saying goodbye? Or taking…" He nodded toward Isaac.

"She went for the weekend to find an apartment. Get a few things in place." She sighed. "And no, apparently she wasn't going to tell you. She was just *not* going to show up for work on Monday morning."

"I can't believe she'd do that to me. What happened? What'd I do?" He leaned toward her, his eyes piercing hers. "Tell me exactly where I can find her."

* * *

Cara stepped out of Justine's car and waved a quick goodbye to her old friend. Then she pulled her sweater tight across her chest to protect herself from the chilly evening wind. As she ran inside through the revolving glass door, she smiled at what a good decision she had made to splurge on herself for once, booking a room at a nice hotel in downtown Chicago instead of in a quieter neighborhood outside the city. The combination of elegant surroundings and wine-induced euphoria made it easier for Cara to forget about New York for a little while.

Tonight, she could take a break from the tangled mess of anger and heartbreak that had surged inside her. Tonight was the start of a new journey. A new life for her and Isaac. They could both move on, go back to their old lives in this familiar city as if they had never left. Ahead of her tomorrow was a long day of touring apartments, and she hoped to sleep well tonight. Unlike last night, when she stared at the clock until three in the morning, crying and unable to calm her mind.

Cara charged through the lobby to the elevator and pressed the button to go upstairs. Then she looked at her watch. It was only ten o'clock. She had time to soak her tired body in the whirlpool tub in her room before relaxing in her luxurious bed for the night.

The elevator arrived quickly. Soon she was on the tenth floor, yawning as she fished for the key in her purse. Her door unlocked with a loud *click*. Immediately, she heard the same loud *click* from the room behind her. She heard the stranger take a few steps into the hall, then stop, as if they were waiting for her. The silence made the hair on the back of her neck stand up.

She pushed her door open, intending to run inside as quickly as possible. Then she heard a voice.

"This is how you break up with me?"

Cara froze, her eyes shut tight. Her stomach did a somersault. *Of course he'd find me...*

"What? No answer?" Victor came up next to her and leaned against the wall outside her door. "I never took you for a coward, Cara. This is what cowards do. They run. You should've given me a chance to explain. Your mom told me you saw a video. It wasn't what you think. It was—"

"It doesn't matter!" Cara opened her eyes, glaring at him. "I'm not stupid. I know she could've rigged that video. I left because I got tired of working someplace where I felt like a pawn in some high school game. Sneaking around, dating my boss, with some jealous psycho ex-girlfriend trying to sabotage me? I need a real job. A real life. I'm doing what's best for me and my son's future."

He smirked softly. "Have you ever thought that maybe *I'm* what's best for you and your son's future?"

Tears filled her eyes. "Victor—"

He put his hands on her shoulders, turning her to face him. "I know what you're thinking. I'm not talking about my money. I'm talking about the way I feel, for both of you."

She did her best to look away. Look anywhere but into his eyes. "I have to go to my room. It's been a long day."

Victor let his arms drop to his sides. "So you're freezing me out?"

Cara pushed her door open and flicked the light switch on the wall. "I'm going to bed."

"Great idea." He rushed after her, letting the door slam shut behind him. "I'm going with you."

She let out a cold laugh as she slung her purse onto the top of the dresser. "I don't think—"

Before she could finish her sentence, he spun her around, smothering her words in a kiss. His hands were everywhere at once, pulling at her clothes as he guided her toward the bed.

A voice inside Cara told her to resist. She didn't make this emergency trip just to give in to him like some flighty, horny teenager.

But then his hand went up her skirt. His lips went to her throat, then trailed warm, wet kisses up to her ear where he whispered, "Don't leave me, Cara."

She grabbed the back of his head. "Victor…"

"Please, *mi preciosa*. Please, stay with me." He withdrew his hand from her skirt and used both hands to quickly unbutton her blouse, immediately pulling it down her arms, along with her sweater. His mouth attached to hers as he reached around her back to unhook her bra.

"Oh!" Cara let out a startled moan as she landed softly—and unexpectedly—on the bed behind her.

Victor tugged at the hem of her stretchy elastic-waist skirt and yanked it down to her shoes. Next came her panties and pantyhose, which he tossed on the floor with the rest of her clothes. Now that she was nude, he fell into bed beside her, his arm sliding under her head to cradle it as he kissed her. His other hand cupped her breast.

Cara's earlier notions of a hot bath and sleep faded away completely as she melted into Victor.

His lips moved from her mouth to her ear, kissing as they went. "I want you," he whispered. "*Mi corazon…*"

And then Cara jolted, as if she was coming out of a trance. "Wait, no. Stop!"

"What?" He pulled away from her immediately.

"Victor." She rolled to her back. "I can't let this happen. You lure me in with your kisses and those sexy Spanish words." She stared up at the ceiling and produced an exasperated sigh. "What are we doing?"

"Well, I don't know what *you're* doing, but I'm doing whatever I can to keep you from getting away. You're obviously not impressed with my money or you wouldn't have left me so easily. I will find a way to make you mine, Cara."

"But, why? You could have any woman you want."

"I know a good thing when I find it. That's why."

Cara hesitated before asking the question she had pondered for days. "But you thought the same thing about Alexis, didn't you? You were going to marry her, and look how that turned out?"

He bristled a little. "Yes. And I've spent a lot of time asking myself the same questions. But now it's so clear. You see, even in the short time I've known you, I've wanted to be with you. Wanted to keep you near where I can see you every day and get to know you more." His head shook gently. "I was never that way with Alexis. I kept myself too busy to see her, and she found comfort with another man. Perhaps it was subconscious, for me. I never really wanted her. I saw her as an investment, I guess, just like everything else in my life. I just wanted to make sure I got married before years went by and I somehow forgot." He paused, softening his voice. "It's completely different with you, Cara. I think of you all the time. I love to just be in your presence. And when I'm not with you, it's only because I've already canceled every meeting I can possibly cancel."

She gulped. "Really? But it seems like you're working all the time."

"I worked much more before you came along." He smiled. "You can ask Gary. He doesn't think I hear him grumbling under his breath about all the changes he has to make to my calendar."

"Oh…" Cara was at a loss for words.

"That's why I simply can't let you get away." Victor leaned down to give her lips a soft kiss. When he pulled away, he propped himself up on his elbow. "So, you must tell me. Is there another reason you came here to Chicago? Is there another man here?"

Cara's eyes widened. "No."

"Really? No competition for me to eliminate?"

"No. There's no one. There hasn't been for years."

"What about Isaac's father? Does he live here?"

"Crap." Cara stared up at the ceiling for a moment, then closed her eyes and hit her forehead with her palm. "I've been dreading this conversation."

"I can see that."

"I didn't tell you this, but I got a card from Alexis a few days ago. She—"

"Why didn't you tell me?" Victor's jaw dropped. "She's

prohibited from contacting you. I would've taken care of it."

"I was afraid, I guess. I don't know."

"She did make a comment to me about it. It was strange and vague. Her last ditch effort to turn me against you, I guess. But I don't believe anything she says."

Cara pulse quickened. "What'd she tell you?"

"That you never told Isaac's father about him."

"What if it's true? Would that turn you against me? After the way you grew up?"

Victor inhaled deeply, a bit of anxiety coursing through him as he considered the question. He immediately thought of his brother Ramon's theories about their father. "There are questions about my father that may never be answered. And my mother, God rest her soul, did the best she could. I believe a child should know his father, if possible. And I think if you decided not to tell Isaac's father, then you must have had a good reason." He cleared his throat. "And if it's okay with you, I'd like to hear that reason."

Relief washed over Cara. She almost laughed, feeling silly that this issue had caused her so much worry. And it was only at this moment she realized just how much she had let it worry her. A nagging sense of dread had lingered in the back of her mind ever since the day Victor first asked about Isaac's paternity. And now it was gone. Still, she stiffened a bit as she collected her thoughts, ready to tell Victor what she had never told anyone before. She took a slow breath and began. "His father was a guy I dated my senior year of college. His name was Marcus. He was a grad student. We met at the beginning of the spring semester that year."

Victor waited patiently as she paused, her face taking on a solemn expression.

She took a moment to collect her thoughts before continuing. "I was a poor student back then. I didn't want more student loans than I already had, so I worked my way through school to pay for living expenses. That semester, the restaurant where I'd waited tables for two years suddenly shut down. Like, overnight. No warning." She sighed. "I really didn't wanna ask Mom for money and get her all worried and worked up. So, I moved in with Marcus after we'd only known each other about a week."

Victor nodded. "Okay."

"At the time I thought it was romantic that he wanted me around so much." She shrugged. "Marcus was so different from any guy I'd ever dated. Very attentive. He'd go out of his way to walk me to class. Take me anywhere I wanted to go, as long as he was with me." She let out a short groan. "He had to know where I was, all the time. And he slowly isolated me from everyone. I couldn't even go to my old roommate's apartment for a girls' night. At first he was sweet about it. He'd talk me into staying home, telling me he wanted to have a romantic evening together. I was the last one to see what was really going on. I felt so stupid. I think it was the fourth time I tried to go out alone, he threw a fit. Broke a chair and told me it was my fault. I made him throw that wooden chair against the wall because I was being so mean to him, you know?"

"That's terrible!"

"Yeah. The guys from upstairs came down to see what the problem was. Marcus calmed right down and told them we were having an argument but we were already making up. I don't know what I said. I think I just stood there in shock. I'd never been scared like that before."

"Did you call the cops?"

Her eyes welled up. "No."

"No? What about your mom? Your friends?"

Cara sniffled, shaking her head. In a thin voice she said, "No."

"You moved out after that, right?"

Tears fell down her face and she wiped them away. "I wish I could say yes. But no. I let another two months go by. What was I supposed to do?" She looked at Victor. "I didn't have a job and he was paying all the bills. If I could just hold on for a little while longer and put up with his temper till graduation I'd never have to see him again."

"But you didn't deserve that. Not for a second. Certainly not for an entire semester."

"I know." Cara turned away from him and took a deep breath to calm down. "I was so ashamed of myself for letting him trick me. I thought he was so nice. I bragged to all my friends about what a great guy I found and then he..." Her voice trailed off. She blinked profusely until her tears were gone, and waited until she could speak without crying. "I remember one night I was in bed, trying to sleep after he'd screamed at me for an hour, accusing me of cheating on him. It was the first time he raised his hand to me. He didn't hit me. He just drew his hand back and acted like he might. He wanted me to be terrified. It reminded me of something my dad told me. He was a cop. He had to deal with domestic violence every day. It really affected him. Especially the women who just didn't wanna leave those men. Sometimes he'd sit me down and have long talks with me, telling me to watch out for these sleaze balls. That's what he'd call 'em, to me. When he didn't know I was listening, he'd call them something much worse."

Victor nodded.

Cara continued. "He'd tell me to always stand up for myself. Never let a man intimidate me. I told him if a man ever hit me I'd kill him. Nothing to worry about. But he explained to me that these guys don't hit their women right away. They wear them down first." She breathed in and out, deeply, trying to keep her tears at bay. "I realized that's what Marcus was doing to me. I can't tell you how stupid I felt. By then, it was hard to get away because he already had so much control over me. He'd check my cell phone all the time to see who I called, who called me. I gave him my email passwords because he blew up at me, accusing me of emailing other guys. I should've just told Mom. She was the one person I was allowed to speak to once in a while without him listening. But I didn't. I wanted her to think everything was okay with me and my nice boyfriend."

"How'd you finally get away?"

"I got sick with a nasty sinus infection and went to the student health center. Found out I was pregnant. I left him the very next day." She shook her head. "Should've left him long before then. But when I found out I was pregnant I knew I couldn't put it off any longer."

"How'd you leave, exactly?"

She sighed. "It was tricky. I had to act like everything was okay that morning. But instead of meeting him after class in our same spot, I went out the other side of the building. Ran to the police station. That night I was sleeping on my old roommate's couch and I had a protective order against Marcus."

"Did he try to contact you again?"

"Yeah. Once. Showed up drunk outside the apartment. Got him arrested for violating the order, *and* for public intoxication."

"And you didn't tell him you were pregnant?"

"No. Didn't tell my friends, either. I didn't want anyone to know it was his baby. I was afraid he might try to get custody if word ever leaked out. So, I waited a good bit after graduation before I told anyone. I made it sound like it was some guy I hooked up with after the break-up. With the timing, my friends probably suspected it was his baby but they never questioned me. Mom never knew about the abuse, so she never questioned it either. Probably figures I had no reason not to tell Marcus."

"Aren't you afraid someone might tell him?"

"No." Her head gently shook. Her eyes became wide. "He's dead."

Victor gasped. "What?"

"Right after we broke up he started drinking a lot more. Dropped out of school. Wasn't long till he got with this girl named Larissa. They were both alcoholics from what I understand. One night in a drunken rage he shot her then shot himself. Isaac was two months old when I found out. I can search for Marcus's name and probably still find the story online."

"Oh my God." Victor's mouth fell open. His eyes wandered around the room as he thought about it. "It's hard to believe sweet little Isaac came from someone with such a gruesome story."

"I know." Cara's eyes were teary again, thinking of her son. "The best thing that ever happened to me came from the worst thing that ever happened to me." She let out a quiet laugh. "I knew he was special the second I learned I was pregnant. I can't describe it. I know it sounds crazy." She wiped her tears away with her hand. "My friends all thought I was insane for wanting to be a single mom right out of college. Going on maternity leave when I wasn't even a year into my first job. But it all worked out, somehow." She breathed a dramatic sigh. "And I'm *so* grateful to have him."

Victor kissed her cheek, then looked at her, grinning. "I'm very grateful you have him, too."

She smirked. "Of course, I say that as I sit in a hotel room eight hundred miles away from him."

He laughed. "It's okay. You need time for yourself once in a while. Doesn't mean you're a bad mother. Besides, you left him in good hands."

"Yeah." Cara frowned as she pictured the heartbroken look on her mother's face that afternoon when she told her she was moving back to Chicago.

He kissed her cheek again, then let his head rest next to hers on the pillow as his arm rested across her bare stomach. His voice was soft in her ear. "I'm going apartment hunting with you tomorrow."

"What?" She rolled over to face him.

"I'm going with you tomorrow. We need to make sure you find just the right apartment. There absolutely *must* be a park nearby where Isaac can play with the neighborhood kids his own age. A nice family-friendly community." His lips pursed, thoughtfully. "You need enough bedrooms for Marcy and Patty to stay comfortably if they visit."

"No, I can't have that many bedrooms in a nice neighborhood. That's three or four times what I was planning to pay—"

"Housing is a benefit of your new consulting job, *querida*." He flashed a wicked grin. "You'll be spending half of your time here, training a new employee to do your old job, and the rest of the time you'll be in New York, with me."

"What? No. My boss, Justine, begged management to get me this job. I'm sure she won't go for that."

"Oh, she will." He nodded. "She'll have no choice, but it'll be best for her and everyone else involved."

Cara raised herself up on her elbows. "Excuse me? How in the world is that possible?"

Chuckling, Victor sat up. "The world's a much smaller place than you think. Especially the business world. I've already made some phone calls. I'll have a meeting or two next week. That's all you need to know."

Cara's mouth gaped in astonishment. "I don't know what to say. Or what to think."

"Listen to me." He cupped her chin. "Now I understand why you're so protective of yourself. Maybe we moved a little too fast and that's why you were so eager to leave me today."

She averted his gaze for a moment, biting her lip.

"It's okay. I'm not upset about it now." His fingers moved to her hair, combing through her soft tendrils until her eyes met his again. "In fact, I think it works out best for everyone. You won't be my employee anymore, technically. You'll be paid by an outside agency. Hopefully you won't feel like you have to sleep with me to keep your job anymore."

Cara's cheeks turned beet red. She tried to suppress her smile, thinking about how exciting it was to sneak around with her boss. Then she breathed deeply to clear her thoughts. "So, you said it works out best for *everyone* this way?"

He returned her smile and gave her lips a quick peck. "Yes. It lets Patty split her time between getting to know her new boyfriend and watching her grandson."

"Yeah. I hadn't thought about that."

"Also, by the time Isaac's ready to start school, you'll hopefully be finished with your project here and you can move home permanently. I know some excellent private schools." Victor nodded. "And this will force us to take our relationship a little slower. That should make you more comfortable, I hope. But, let me warn you." His eyes narrowed as his voice took on a slightly sinister tone. "On those days when I get you all to myself, I will be very greedy."

Cara giggled into Victor's mouth as it descended on hers.

His warm hand cupped her full breast as his lips moved to her chin, then her throat. His hand was moving down her stomach to part her thighs when he heard her groan. He stopped. "What's wrong?"

She winced, painfully. "I'm sorry. There's this nagging thought running through my mind. Alexis. Will she bother me here? What if—"

"Shh." He pressed two fingers against her lips. "I have something very special planned for her. She'll get what she deserves. Let's not speak of her again." His lips went to her ear as his fingers trailed down her neck, her chest, her stomach, stopping between her thighs. "I have something *much* more special planned for you, *mi amor*."

Cara closed her eyes, pleasure coursing through her body from his wet, warm lips nibbling her ear, and the words he had just spoken. She knew *amor* meant love, and that was a word they hadn't yet used with each other.

As if he could read her thoughts, he moaned in her ear as the tips of his fingers traced circles around her tiny, swollen nub. "I'm falling in love with you, Cara. Please don't run from me again."

Before she could say, "I won't," his mouth possessed hers again with a fiery kiss that resonated throughout every part of her body, increasing the pleasure he was building in her pelvis. She bucked against his hand, needing more.

He continued to kiss and fondle her, enjoying her cries of joy that were quieted by his mouth until they were so loud and frequent, he was forced to break the kiss. He watched as her mouth fell open and her face made the most gorgeous expressions of pleasure he had ever seen. *I hope to see this beautiful sight a million more times…*

A minute later, as Cara lay there recovering, Victor yawned and let his head fall to the same pillow where she rested. His arm went gently across her stomach, holding her close.

She opened her eyes, startled. "You're going to sleep already?"

With a satisfied smile, he whispered, "We need to rest. We have a long day ahead of us but I plan to wake you *very* early. And very happily."

"Okay." Cara giggled quietly as his lips gently touched her forehead.

CHAPTER SEVENTEEN

Alexis clutched the note in her hand, reading it for perhaps the hundredth time since it was delivered to her house with a bouquet of roses the day before.

I've missed you, mi amor. My body endlessly longs for yours. Put me out of my misery. Pack your bags and come with me to my secret island paradise. We will spend a week alone and put the past far, far behind us.

Kisses,

Your Latin Lover

Also attached were instructions to board the Monarch Enterprises private jet at promptly six-thirty the next morning. And Alexis did so, without question.

The three hour flight passed quickly. Alexis was alone in the plane's cabin with champagne, magazines, and movies to keep her busy. Most of her time was spent re-reading the note and fantasizing about Victor. She was determined not to make him feel badly about the past few months. He had finally come to his senses, just like she knew he would all along. He had to find a lover to rebound after their break-up. But Cara Green was now living in Chicago, and today's trip was obvious proof that the relationship was over. *All it took was a little distance…* Alexis smiled proudly at how well her hard work had paid off.

It must have been when I jumped in his arms…he couldn't stop thinking about me, holding me and loving me again. The thought made her giddy.

But a chill of concern crawled up her spine when the plane landed and she took notice of the tiny airport. Something wasn't right. The dusty old building was small and unkempt, practically rural. It looked so desolate beside the beautiful blue ocean.

The pilot smiled and helped load her bags into the back of an old Jeep and said something in Spanish to the driver before turning back to the jet.

"Wait!" Alexis stood outside the vehicle, afraid to get in.

"Yes?" The pilot turned around.

"Is this safe?" With a hand over her eyes to block out the sun, Alexis nodded toward the long dirt road where the vehicle was set to drive. The road was narrow and winding, running parallel to the ocean and disappearing a short way off in the distance.

The pilot gave the area a quick glance. "Yes, it'll be fine. The driver's taking you to a villa a few miles away."

"Oh." Alexis smiled. "So, this is Victor Barboza's private island?"

"Something like that. I don't know the details. I *do* know we have a trip scheduled to pick you up in a week unless otherwise notified. You can leave earlier if someone radios the mainland." He started toward his plane, and over his shoulder nodded quickly at Alexis and said, "Good day, ma'am."

Someone has to radio the mainland to get me out of here?

Startled by this revelation, she hesitantly took a seat in the back of the Jeep. The driver stepped on the gas, kicking up dirt and gravel under their wheels just as she was pulling out her cell phone. No signal. She continued to stare at it, waiting for those lines to appear. Her eyes were often distracted by the beautiful deep blue ocean to her right. To her left, the landscape was dotted with rocks and sand and the occasional ramshackle hut.

Alexis tapped on the driver's shoulder. "Where are you taking me? How much farther?"

The driver shook his head and pointed up the road, uttering a word that sounded like, "*Cuanto.*"

A few minutes later they rounded a corner and there was a building—the first structure that looked at least semi-habitable to Alexis. It resembled a giant sandcastle, but there were tropical trees in front of it, and it had walls that looked sturdy and well-built.

Alexis exhaled with great relief. When the vehicle stopped, she jumped out, leaving the driver to carry her bags to the door as she ran toward the building, her heart pounding furiously as she anticipated the opulence awaiting her with Victor inside.

As she reached the door, she heard a familiar voice from the side of the building.

"*Alexis, mi amor!*"

Oh no. She turned to the bare-chested man she saw running toward her out of the corner of her eye.

Esteban.

Her mind reeled as she attempted to process the situation with a gleeful Esteban rambling away in front of her. Their affair ended soon after Victor caught them together. Alexis hadn't seen Esteban in several months.

"*Mi princesa, mi amor. He esperado mucho por ti. Vamos adentro. Quiero llenarte de besos placenteros…*"

Alexis slowly began to cry as she watched the driver silently carry her bags inside the dwelling.

"What is wrong?" Esteban put his hands on her shoulders, a sweet look of concern on his tanned, chiseled face. "You don't want to be here?"

"Um…I…um…"

"Oh, *mi amor*." He took one of her hands and placed it against his smooth, bare chest. His voice was soft. "My heart wants you. *Perdona…*" He stopped and let out a grunt of frustration. "My English suffers, *mi amor*. The locals, they speak Spanish."

"Locals?"

Alexis nodded along as Esteban switched between the two languages, telling her the story of this island. The best she could understand, there was a village on another island nearby, but Esteban stayed here where he had worked as Victor's groundskeeper for the past two months.

"So sorry," Esteban said. "You would not talk to me. I call you, you hang up. You change your number. I visit your house, they say 'she not here.' And next time, police take me away. I had to leave the city. So painful to me, losing you. I was desperate. I meet with Victor. He forgive me for my," his eyes darted around as he searched for the correct word, "*indiscretion* with you. He give me job far, far away from the city." His full lips formed a distinct frown; his hand went to her hair. "Away from you, like you want."

Alexis felt the warmth of his fingers as they weaved into the tendrils around her ear. She swallowed, hard. "I see."

He gently shook his head. "You want to go?" He glanced at the driver, who stood close by waiting for a signal to stay or leave. "You may go somewhere. He take you to boat. I know nice people on other island where you stay. I arrange. You leave tomorrow."

Alexis was slightly dizzy, overwhelmed by the shock of the

situation, and the decision before her. She remembered how painful it was to ignore Esteban, but she had convinced herself it would lead to a future with Victor. She forced herself to forget Esteban, and it was easy once he stopped pursuing her. But now, she knew why he stopped. She told herself at the time that it didn't matter, that Esteban was crazy for stalking her for weeks after she told him it was over. After recent events, she felt a twinge of sympathy.

His gorgeous face and rock hard chest were framed by an endless blue sky. He was sexier than ever, but he was so sad. His eyes dropped to the sandy ground below them, only looking up when she finally spoke.

"Esteban." Several large tears ran down Alexis's face. "I will stay here, with you."

His face lit up. "Yes? With me?" He quickly signaled at the driver to leave, then took both of her hands in his. "Oh, *mi amor*. You make me so happy." He chatted on, extending his arm behind him, speaking in a frantic line of broken English that Alexis could barely follow. After a little while, he stopped and said, "*Perdona*. Too much talk. Few visitors. Lonely sometimes. But now," he brought her hand to his mouth and kissed it, "you are here."

Alexis wiped her tears away as Esteban hooked his arm around hers, escorting her into the house as he rambled on about the fish he caught this morning that he would later cook for dinner. *If I can handle these rustic surroundings, maybe I'll stay longer than a week.*

* * *

Six Months Later

The music started. Tom took a deep breath and glanced

down the wide aisle between the pews at the church, his trembling hands folded in front of him.

The best man—his son, Gregory—patted his father on the back and whispered near his ear, "Don't look so nervous. I got a guy waitin' in the parking lot if she tries to run."

Tom smiled. He was grateful to his son for easing the tension. He felt like such a fool for being so anxious. A few minutes earlier, he had looked at his reflection in the mirror and laughed at the old man staring back at him. White hair, white mustache, all very neatly groomed. Wearing a tuxedo that—in his mind—was meant for a fresh-faced man half his age. But today, Tom felt like a giddy young man as he waited not-so-patiently for his blushing bride.

It was a small wedding of exactly fifty-five guests, to be followed by a reception in a hotel ballroom a few blocks away. Originally, Patty only wanted to elope, but planning the wedding gave her something to do on the weeks when Isaac and Cara weren't around. As of two weeks earlier, they were living with her again, and Patty was thrilled. But now that Tom would be moving in with Patty, Cara and Isaac were planning a move to Manhattan to live with Victor and give the newlyweds their privacy.

Patty stood in the back and watched Marcy walk down the aisle in her lime green chiffon dress—a dress that Marcy was skeptical of at first, but today she looked gorgeous. The color brought out Marcy's hazel eyes and looked beautiful with the thick chocolate-colored curls that hung down her back. Patty was determined to find a man for Marcy, and soon.

Cara turned around and gave her mother one last kiss on the cheek, then stood back to make sure she had left no lipstick on her skin. "I love you, Mom."

Patty's eyes welled up. She could only smile and nod, afraid that speaking would cause a torrent of tears to flood her cheeks.

Cara looked down at Isaac, the ring bearer, and said, "Remember, count to ten before you walk out."

Isaac nodded. He had already peeked inside the sanctuary at all the people sitting there, and he was nervous. *What if I drop this pillow?* But then he remembered what Victor said. *The rings on the pillow are fake. Don't let all the people scare you. Just walk down the aisle and find me on the front row. After this is over, we can eat cake.*

Isaac felt a lot better when he thought about that cake. And he knew Grandma had made the cake herself, so it would be extra good. She even let Isaac pick the flavor: chocolate. He tensed a little when he felt Grandma patting his shoulder, urging him to enter the room full of people; he had forgotten to count to ten.

When Isaac entered the room, it felt so much bigger than it had when it was empty. The people inside were all dressed so nice, all of them smiling and pointing at him. Some of them waved. He smiled and waved back at a woman he recognized as Grandma's neighbor, but the pillow almost fell to the floor. "No!" Isaac gasped and quickly shuffled the pillow back into place, safely resting it in his arms. He saw Mommy grinning at him from the front of the church, and he grinned back at her, then started to walk a little faster than before. When he got closer to the end of the aisle, he saw Victor waving from the front row.

Victor scooted over and patted the empty space on the pew, then patted Isaac's back when he sat down. "Good job."

Isaac gave him a big smile.

And then the music changed. Victor said, "Come on. Let's stand up and watch Grandma walk down the aisle."

Throughout the ceremony, Victor couldn't take his eyes off Cara. She was stunning in her dress. A true vision to behold. Everything about her was lovely, both inside and out. He put a friendly arm around Isaac's shoulders as he contemplated how lucky he was to have found this amazing woman and her amazing son, and how much better they had both made his life. Soon, Victor would tell Cara that he was going to stop putting in so much time at work. He had invested well, and he wanted to spend more time with the people he loved, not in stuffy board rooms in endless meetings.

Victor would take Cara home to Texas, show her the beauty of the landscape and introduce her to the friends and family he loved so well. The ring purchased five months earlier would finally come out of its hiding place, and they'd take the next step in their lifelong journey together.

He would take Isaac to the ranch where he grew up, and have Ramon show him around. Horses beat fast cars any day of the week. At least, that's what Victor was counting on.

His gaze caught Cara's for a moment. He saw the same look in Patty's eyes during her vows. That look was something special. It would last. It would be Victor's, for the remaining days of his life.

The End

Follow the continuing story of the Barboza Brothers in Book Two: **Armando Returns**.

Sign up to receive an email when book two is available at **http://www.reeniaustin.com**

CONTACT REENI

Facebook: **http://www.facebook.com/ReeniAustin**
Email: **http://www.reeniaustin.com/contact**

Page intentionally left blank...